+
W669f

Finding
David
Dolores

Also by Margaret Willey

The Bigger Book of Lydia

HARPER & ROW, PUBLISHERS   NEW YORK

Cambridge
Philadelphia
San Francisco
London
Mexico City
São Paolo
Singapore
Sydney

Finding
David
Dolores

Margaret
Willey

Library of Congress Cataloging-in-Publication Data
Willey, Margaret.
   Finding David Dolores.

   Summary: Thirteen-year-old Arly's private obsession
with an older boy, the mysterious David Dolores,
becomes complicated when she makes friends with an
eccentric, demanding new girl in town.
   [1. Friendship—Fiction.   2. Parent and child—
Fiction]   I. Title.
PZ7.W65548Fi 1986   [Fic]   85-45252
ISBN 0-06-026483-7
ISBN 0-06-026484-5 (lib. bdg.)

*for my parents, Barbara
and Foster Willey*

Finding
David
Dolores

One

When I think of the spring when I first saw David Dolores, I remember the way I used to wander through the town of St. Martins like someone lost, a solitary, ungrounded silhouette, drifting through mist and rain. Even in clear sunshine I wandered around in a kind of fog—in my memories I'm like a blur in the background of a photograph, hard to see unless one is looking for what doesn't belong.

I was thirteen that year, the year of my transformation into what my mother called a woman. But only a fool, I thought, would have called me a woman then. I was neither girl nor woman, old nor young, and I was at odds with all the expectations that come with growing up. And my mother had become the person who upset me the most because she still presumed to know what was happening to me—and what I should do about it.

Before that year we had been as close as any mother and daughter can be. She had enjoyed telling people that I was her best friend. But that year hearing this made me furious. I was pulling away from her and she refused to see it. My goal in life was to avoid her.

I began taking aimless, solitary walks, away from her, away from my dull neighborhood and from my old girlfriends, whose lives seemed utterly unconnected to mine. I wore my loneliness proudly, like a banner, and guarded my privacy fiercely, as though my life was full of important secrets.

My mother kept struggling to stay in touch with me. She decided that I needed new grown-up clothes, and went out on her own to buy me cowgirlish ruffled skirts and plaid blouses, which were the latest style. She'd always loved buying clothes for me, but now I refused to be interested. I was wearing only clothes that hid my body, as I hid all the rest of me. My closet was full of loose-fitting corduroys and worn flannel shirts and comfortable walking shoes. When my mother refused to buy the kind of clothes I wanted, I bought them myself with my allowance at secondhand shops.

"What are you trying to prove by looking like some sort of orphan?" my mother cried in dismay. "You're a beautiful young *woman*, Arleena!"

"I am not!" I answered. "Are you blind?"

I suppose to her I might have somehow looked beautiful. But now I was thin and lanky and I had a ridiculously long neck. My hair was wiry, like the hair on the head of an old doll, always rumpled. I gave up trying to control it and instead spent hours in front of my bedroom mirror arranging my face into an expression that was both aloof and proud, squinting and keeping my mouth in a line, with my head up high.

My father had an easier time leaving me alone than my mother did. He owned a music store downtown, and he was always busy, working with the local schools, placing instruments with high school students. And because we had never been close in the same way as Mother and I, he had a certain neutrality that I needed.

"Just let her be," he would advise my mother gently, and then he would ask me to take it easy on her.

"She sees you're growing up and she misses you," he'd say.

"God, she asks me a million questions a day," I'd complain.

"Answer one or two, then, Arly," he'd suggest. "It won't kill you."

He accepted the deliberate neglect of my clothes and hair. But even he expressed some concern about what Mother called my scowling.

"I can't help wondering if you can see all right. With all that . . . squinting."

5

"I see fine," I insisted, lifting my chin. "This is me. This is how I look."

And the expression worked. At school everyone grew wary of me and treated me like someone who prefers solitude. Slowly, in the course of that year, I cleared a path through my confusion and traveled it urgently, wandering through St. Martins in the afternoons and late at night, through the ravines in the mornings before school, or along the rough, empty beaches at sunset.

Then in the spring, in March, when the town was gray and wet, but full of expectancy and the sounds of melting ice, I first saw him—David Dolores. Just like that—overnight—I found a purpose. And a destination.

Two

My statue stood on the bluff overlooking St. Martins' channel. Fireman Joseph was ten feet high, his coat flailing, his body hunched as though charging forward. One of his huge arms shielded his helmeted head, the other held a small cat-sized girl, who was clinging to his chest, her mouth a beseeching O.

He was my favorite statue, a tribute to the firemen killed in an opera hall across the river, which had burned to the ground. I visited Fireman Joseph all that year, especially late at night, when my parents thought I was asleep in my bed. The lights from the river would light up his shiny surface, giving him an unearthly glow.

On the morning I first saw David Dolores, it was raining lightly, and a circle of ivy and trillium had bloomed at the base of the statue. I felt suddenly that things in my life would get better. I started for home, enjoying the rain, when just ahead of me I noticed an older boy, walking east and crisscrossing my route home. It seemed almost as though we were the only people out in the rain that spring morning.

Maybe, I thought, he was just out wandering, like me. I followed him. He was very tall and erect, wearing a black poncho that flapped behind him like a cape, although his head was bare. His hair was long for a boy and combed back, so that it fell in a blue-black sheet to the base of his neck. His face was very white, elegant and chiseled, and he had thick, dark eyebrows. His mouth was set in a line, and he held his head up with a kind of deliberate aloofness that I recognized as my own. But he was much more elegant than I could ever be.

I followed him for nearly two more miles until finally, as I watched from a block away, he walked up the front stairs of a huge white house and disappeared inside. It was an old house, Victorian, with a twin-pillared porch, a gable, and three tall arched windows across the front. The door had an oval of stained glass that refracted light as it opened and closed. I thought I heard a momentary flurry of music from within and

8

caught one tall shadow moving across the front windows.

Oh, God, I whispered, drifting back to the edges of my own neighborhood. *At last I've found someone.*

The next day was a Sunday, so I went back to the house on Langley, walked by the front porch and circled the yard. Enclosed by a waist-high picket fence was a sprawling, unkempt rectangle of property, lined with apple and cherry trees. In one corner was a half circle of rosebushes, a plaster birdbath at the center. Bird feeders were everywhere—grain stations, wren houses, suet attached to trees, and drip buckets hanging from branches.

At the back of the yard, closest to me, was a dilapidated garage with one small window facing the rear of the house. I pushed on the door—it was unlocked. Inside I found an abandoned workshop with rusted paint cans, a few tools, and a waist-high stack of newspapers. I stood at the streaked window, rubbed a circle clean, and saw that I had a clear view of the back door of the house.

I waited half an hour, until I grew restless. To my left, inside the fence, I could see a trash container full of newspapers and magazines. I slipped out of the garage and ducked along the fence, reaching over the slats to grab some magazines from the top of the canister. I carried them to the edge of the ravine and sat down. The first was a jazz magazine called *Cadence.*

It was addressed to a David Dolores. *David*, I whispered. The second was *Bird-Watchers Digest*, also addressed to him. *American Quilting* was the third magazine, addressed to an Althea Dolores. I cast it aside and returned my attention to the first two, flipping through them reverently until I was too cold to sit outside any longer. Then I carried them home, slipped them under my coat at the door, and hurried to my room.

My mother heard me come in. She called to me from her office off the kitchen. She was correcting exams for the anthropology classes she taught for a small local college.

"Arleena, could you come here a minute?"

I winced, put the two magazines under my bed, and went to her office doorway. She put a stack of papers aside and smiled at me.

"Where've you been, honey?" she asked.

"Out," I said. "Walking."

She sighed. "Out walking, is it, my little refugee? You didn't have to go alone, you know."

I didn't answer.

"Well, comb your hair and get ready to help me make supper."

"Call me when you need me," I said, and hurried back to my room, uncomfortable at the thought of having to work in the kitchen. My mother was an excellent cook and my own clumsiness in her domain bewildered her.

Back in my room I took out a map of St. Martins and studied it, placing a red X on Langley, where David's house was. Then I noticed that the ravine behind the Dolores property was part of a trio of ravines that ran through the east end of town, cutting an arc that started just north of my street. *A secret route,* I thought, full of excitement. When my mother called, I sighed, put the map under my bed with the magazines, and dragged myself to the kitchen.

She was kneading dough for pasta. "Come on," she urged. "I want to talk to you."

"What about?" I asked.

"About you," she said. "Tell me what you've been up to. You've been out of the house all weekend."

"What do you want me to help you with?" I asked impatiently.

"Get the paring knife and chop an onion," she said. "And tell me what you did all weekend."

"I *told* you," I said, opening and closing drawers. "I tell you and then you ask me *again.*" I dropped the onion and it rolled across the floor, toward her. She picked it up and handed it back to me with a sigh.

"All right, all right," she said. "Never mind. Watch your fingers."

She was quiet a minute. Then she cleared her throat. "Do any homework yet, Arleena?" she asked, trying to sound nonchalant.

I gritted my teeth. "I have all night to do it. I don't have very much."

"You never used to leave everything till the last possible minute," she said quietly. "Then you wonder why your grades are slipping."

"I don't wonder," I insisted. "I *know* why. Didn't we already talk about this, Mom?"

"We haven't talked about *anything* in weeks, Arleena," she complained. Then she tried to sound more cheerful. "I just have one little suggestion. I found this article in a magazine about helping your kids to pace their homework better. You set up a work schedule with certain times every evening . . ."

She went on describing the article, but I wasn't listening. In my head I was planning to explore the ravines the next day, to trace a path to the gully behind the Dolores property.

"Well, what do you think, Arleena?" my mother asked, interrupting my thoughts. "Does it make sense to you?"

"Sounds fine," I said, too quickly.

She glared at me, realizing I hadn't been listening. Lately she'd been trying different ways to get me to talk about school. My cryptic remarks about various classes and teachers upset her; she believed in schools and classrooms and was a popular, dedicated teacher. The few times we'd talked about it had been unsuccessful—she wanted specific complaints and clear examples of what was bothering me, but what I felt was much more sweeping than I could explain. It was all the routine, the schedules, the sameness combined with the expectations of strangers who didn't understand me.

The onion slipped, and I nicked the tip of one finger and swore.

"Wash it with soap," my mother instructed in a disappointed voice, and I slipped away.

The next week I explored the ravines after school. It was March, and the gullies were stark and empty of leaves, so it was easy to make my way, even in the places where there were no paths. I kept track of my progress, marking trees and fallen logs with a penknife, wanting to know all the routes before the summer when the landscape would become a tangled and overgrown jungle.

Then on Saturday, after waiting for an hour at the grimy window of the garage behind David Dolores' house, I saw him again. He stepped out of the back door, waving good-bye to someone inside. He wore the same poncho, but this time he carried an instrument case in one hand and held a small portfolio under the opposite arm. He walked in the same princely manner, and I watched spellbound for a few moments before I shot out of the garage to follow him. He walked down Langley and I walked parallel to him on Monroe, watching him on the side streets, glad that he kept his eyes straight ahead. Half a mile from his house he turned east, past me, down Wilbur Avenue, and now I could walk directly behind him. After a few more blocks he walked up to a small one-story house and rang the doorbell. Once he was inside, I crossed the street and entered an abandoned warehouse. Under a broken window, I sat on a cement stairway, shivering. I was wondering how long David would be inside the house across the street when the faint, solemn sound of an oboe came floating up. I didn't recognize the music then, didn't even know what an oboe was, but I imagined how majestic the sight of David playing whatever he was playing must be. I listened for half an hour, then watched from the window as David left the house and headed back toward Langley. I drifted happily back home, to the privacy of my own room, where I pulled the map out from under my bed and put an X on Wilbur Avenue, then traced a red line from Langley. *Music Lesson*, I wrote on a sheet of paper that I'd stapled to the map. *Saturdays. Three o'clock.*

Some afternoons I waited at the bus stop on the corner of Langley and Park for David to pass by me on his way home from high school. He never looked at any of the younger students, so it was easy for me to stare at him. The weather grew warmer and he often wore a manly, dark-green sweater-jacket, or sometimes a Mexican-looking pullover with a hood. He also wore white jeans with black shoes—an odd combination that made him look like he was wearing clothes from some other country. His face was always the same—olive-shaped eyes, dark eyebrows, a long, angular chin held high. He seemed so much older than the other high school students, like a grown man. How I wished that I could walk the way he did, so majestically. My face in the bedroom mirror seemed wispy and insignificant, and yet knowing David existed made me feel more important somehow.

Our junior high library had copies of the high school yearbooks. I found the most recent and located David's picture amid the juniors. That meant he was a senior this year. The librarian let me take the yearbook home, and in my own room I again examined the tiny photograph of David. Even in the stiff artificial pose of a class picture, he looked sophisticated. I resisted the impulse to rip out the page.

There were other pictures of him. One for the swim team—a group photograph in which his sleek head towered behind the white torsos of the swimmers in the front row. Then I found him seated in a group portrait of the senior symphony with a complicated instrument resting on his lap. It looked like a clarinet, but slightly different. In this picture, David's face was poised and elegant. I closed the book and took it to where my father was reading the newspaper.

"Look here," I said, reopening the yearbook and pointing to the instrument in David's lap. "What instrument is that, Dad?"

"It looks like an oboe," he said. Then he peered more closely. "Hmmm, I know that boy," he added mildly.

"You *do*?" I exclaimed.

"I can't think of his name. He buys reeds at the

15

shop. I hear he's very talented. Why do you ask?"

I closed the book abruptly. "I just wanted to know what that instrument was," I mumbled.

My father put his newspaper down and leaned toward me. "Are you interested in playing the oboe, Arly?" he asked.

I shrugged. "I might be," I said evasively. "In the future."

"Well, you let me know, Arly," he said. "I could bring you one home from the shop and you could try it out—see if you like it. You just let me know."

I nodded and left the room quickly. My mother would have been ecstatic if I showed an interest in playing an instrument.

The next night when I came home from school there was an oboe from Dad's shop on my bed in a battered case. I looked it over and then put it under my bed with my other David Dolores material.

The same week, I approached the junior and senior high school music teacher, Ed Watkins, a pleasant man who was a friend of my father's. I told him I might be interested in playing the oboe, and his eyebrows raised in approval.

"Is there anyone in the high school symphony who is a good oboe player?" I asked innocently.

His eyebrows lifted again. "It just so happens that we have the best oboe player in the state," he announced proudly.

"Really?" I asked. "What's his name?"

"The Dolores boy," he said. "David."

It took my breath away to hear his name pronounced. I waited a few seconds and then asked the first question that came into my mind about David's family.

"What does his father do?"

Ed Watkins looked surprised.

"I was just wondering," I explained, "if his father is a musician, too."

Mr. Watkins' expression remained somewhat bewildered. "He might have been," he mused, half to himself. Then he looked back at me. "This particular boy's father is not living. Just his mother. Anyway, what . . . when do you plan to start with the oboe, Arly?"

"Next year," I said. "I'm a little too busy to start now." I hurried away, wanting to think; the new information was disturbing. Was this tragedy what had made him seem so adult, so manly?

For days I thought about him in this light, following him after school with new zeal. It was easy for me to believe he was the best musician around. Just seeing him at a distance had filled me with hope.

I now had a bedroom full of maps and notes, a few copies of *Cadence*, several library books on ornithology, and an oboe. I bought film for my father's long-unused Instamatic and took a series of photographs, from the edge of the ravine, of David leaving his house. The pictures were quite blurry and dim. But the fact that I had taken them secretly, unnoticed, made my life seem very full somehow. And yet, it was a strange

17

energy that infused me, because where other people were concerned, my life had never been emptier. Sometimes I went for days without ever really speaking to anyone.

Three

That same spring a new seventh grader came to our junior high. Her name was Regina, and she pronounced this coldly, introducing herself to the class without smiling. She was tall and broad shouldered, and on her first day at Central she wore a dark-red silk dress with padded shoulders and matching shoes with a three-inch wedge. The girls at my school dressed mostly in jeans and oxford-cloth blouses, and nobody tall would have dared to wear heels. Regina had waist-length, straight blond hair and piercingly blue eyes. Despite my own disinterest in clothes, I was impressed with her worldly and superior air. I watched her for the next few days. The other kids seemed intimidated by her. Whenever she spoke in class, it was with a tone of heavy sarcasm, as though our school was a huge disappointment to her. We assumed she was from a big city school or a private school. She was obviously too sophisticated for the likes of Central.

By her second week I was so curious that I slipped into line behind her in the cafeteria. She was sneering at a plate of tuna and noodles on her plastic tray.

"It's a crime, isn't it," I said apologetically, "what they try to pass off as food in this school."

Regina looked down at me, faintly suspicious. Then she sighed. "Well, I for one will *not* pretend that this is edible."

"I have some quiche that my mother made," I offered. "You could have a piece of it."

Regina considered this for a moment, then nodded and followed me back to my table.

"You're used to a better school than Central, aren't you?" I asked as we sat down together.

"Yes, I am," Regina said. Then she added, "These little midwestern schools are all the same."

"Where are you from?"

"Oh, I've lived all over. When I was growing up my father sold insurance. The last school I was at was in Minneapolis." She sighed. "I could practically write a book on comparative school systems."

I shook my head, impressed. "Well," I said, "at least

20

you've had some variety. That's more than I can say. What do you think of Central?"

Regina reached for her tray and lifted a cold gob of discarded tuna and noodles with her fork. She pointed to it with her other hand. "See this?" she asked me. "This is what I think of Central."

The next day I looked for her again in the cafeteria. She was eating alone, as I often did, and she looked up as I approached her. She pushed her long bangs out of her eyes and gave me a fleeting, wary smile.

"I never told you my name yesterday," I said, sitting down across from her. "It's Arly Weston."

"Hi, Arly," Regina said. The same smile. "I thought I might have been too insulting yesterday. About your school."

"Oh, I don't think of it as *my* school, Regina," I objected. "I agree with what you said. I'd give anything to be able to switch to a better school. What was it like to go to school in a big city like Minneapolis?"

Regina leaned forward, pleased. "It was the most wonderful place, Arly. I mean, it wasn't even set up like a regular school—it was a group of students who went all over the city, to a different place each day— museums, galleries, ethnic restaurants, libraries. I absolutely loved it." Regina was smiling now, without a trace of cynicism. Then her face drooped a little. "It spoiled me, actually. It made it that much harder to move here."

21

"Your dad again?" I wondered.

Regina scowled. "No," she said. "My mother. My dad lives in California now. She wanted to come here because she'd lived here as a child or something. I don't know."

"God," I sympathized. "It must be murder to be here after going to a school like the one in Minneapolis."

"Oh, it is," Regina agreed glumly. "It's terrible. I could just kill her for it." She looked around the lunchroom and sighed. "I can see that I'm not going to, as they say, *fit in*, here at Central. You're the first person who's been the least bit friendly. Of course, these kids are pretty small-townish, aren't they? They're all busy trying to outdo each other being ordinary. Know what I mean?"

I nodded, hiding my excitement that she would confide in me. I wanted suddenly to confide in turn.

"I just *hate* this place, Regina," I whispered across the table. "More every day."

Regina rolled her eyes sympathetically. "But, you know, I keep telling myself if there wasn't school to go to, I'd have to stay *home*. Which would be one hundred times worse." She threw up her hands. "Our wonderful teen years, Arly. Isn't it a laugh?"

Lunch hour was over, and Regina stood up and brushed the crumbs off her black miniskirt.

"Oops, I'm late for biology," she said. "The absolute *highlight* of my day. See you tomorrow?" I watched her walk away with a leather bag on one shoulder and

22

her blond ponytail swinging. She walked slowly, deliberately, as heads turned and groups stopped talking along the path she cut between the tables with her long legs.

I was thrilled with Regina. She was so dramatic. She would gesture with her hands as she spoke, sweeping her arms like a dancer. She could dismiss the entire population of my school with one curl of her lip. But she seemed to really like *me*. We would sit at lunch with our heads together, giggling with shared disdain. After we had done this for two weeks, Regina missed one lunch hour completely. I looked for her after school and found her walking along the corridor outside the gymnasium.

"Regina!" I called. She turned and looked relieved to see me. "Where were you at lunchtime?"

"Oh, Arly. I couldn't face the cafeteria today. I had the most wretched morning. Mr. Baker insulted me in front of the entire math class."

"What did he say?"

"He took one look at my outfit and then announced that Central Junior High is not Hollywood." Regina was wearing a short pink sweat-shirt dress with black beads, hose, and earrings.

I laughed, but Regina didn't join me. "Oh, God, Arly, it was so insulting! I wanted to scream."

"Did you say anything back to him?"

"I told him that I'd *noticed*. Then later I thought of a million better things to say. I can't get it out of my head. I am so fed up. Nobody appreciates a little style in this awful place!"

"Just forget it, Regina," I said. "Tell yourself that school will be over with in just another six weeks."

This didn't cheer her at all. "What's the difference?" she grumbled. "I don't even know this wretched town. I don't belong here. I might as well be on the moon."

"Regina," I asked gently, "does your mother know how much you hate St. Martins?"

She grimaced. "I can't explain anything to her, Arly. It's like talking to a wall."

"I know what you mean," I said. "My mom's the same way."

We had come to the corner where I always turned and cut through the ravines to David's bus stop.

"Oh, walk with me a little farther," Regina pleaded, surprising me. "I've had such an awful day, and I won't see anyone civilized again until Monday."

I had planned to look for David, but I was pleased.

"Sure," I agreed, thinking that I could just as easily see David the next day. We walked a little farther, and then Regina pointed to a small gray house a block away.

"That's my house," she announced quietly. She seemed all the more discouraged. I tried to think of something to say that would help, but she was moving away from me, toward her house, waving glumly.

"Regina!" I called impulsively. "Let's do something

24

tomorrow. Let's just hang around together or something."

Regina smiled. "Okay," she called back. "Where do you live?"

"On Court Street," I yelled. "I'll come to your house and get you. At eleven!"

Regina shook her head. "Meet me at this corner," she insisted, pointing to the street sign next to where I stood. "I'll be waiting for you."

The outside of Regina's house had surprised me. It was a ranch-style gray box with aluminum siding, a white door, plain windows. I had expected Regina to live in a house that was more unusual. But Regina had actually agreed to spend a Saturday with me. I felt myself on the verge of an important friendship. By the time I rushed into my own kitchen, I was brimming with excitement.

"What's with you?" my mother asked. "You look as though you're about to explode. Did you get a good grade on your algebra exam?"

"There's this new girl at school that I've been hanging around with, Mom," I burst out. "We're going to do something together tomorrow."

"That's terrific, Arleena!" my mother said enthusiastically. "What's her name?"

"Regina Miller."

"Is she a good student?" This was generally the first question my mother asked.

25

"Oh, God yes," I said. "She's the smartest girl in our class."

My mother brightened. "Why don't you girls have lunch here?" she suggested. "I could make a soufflé!"

"Oh, we're having lunch at her house," I said quickly. "Maybe next time."

"What about supper?" she was calling, but I hurried to my room and shut the door.

Four

Regina was at the street sign the next day, wearing faded jeans and a knee-length striped sweater, her hair in a long braid. She was hungry, so the first place we walked to was a downtown diner that served the best hamburgers in St. Martins. Then we headed toward the river. All along the way I told her things that I knew about St. Martins, pointing out some of the oldest buildings downtown and the historic sites along the bluff. I watched Regina's face as I talked, afraid of finding a bored expression, but it was an exhilarating, clear spring day and the river was rushing crazily and Regina was relaxed and wide-eyed.

We headed west along the river toward a deserted stretch of riverbank, flat except for a few small scrub bushes and patches of dogwood. Before us the river churned and shimmered into shallow rapids.

"God, this is a beautiful spot!" Regina exclaimed. "How did you know how to get down here?"

"I discovered the path last fall," I explained. "One of the things I do after school is look for special places like this."

"I've never been in a town long enough to get interested in special places," said Regina, partly to herself. She looked at me. "You know so many things about St. Martins, Arly."

I was flattered. "There are other places I could show you," I suggested. Then I added, "Some people think it's a strange way to spend time, though."

"Who thinks it's strange?" Regina wondered.

I shrugged. "My mother."

"Your mother!" Regina scoffed. "Who cares? My mother thinks every single move I make is strange!"

"I guess the girls I used to hang around with think it's weird, too. Rita Mellendorf and Kay Maxwell and that whole group. I can tell."

"Who *cares*!" Regina exclaimed again. "If you ask me, Arly, those girls are pathetic!"

She picked up two large rocks and hoisted them up on her broad shoulders like a weightlifter. "Now pretend this is Rita and this is Kay," she said, mock serious, while I giggled. Then she gave a huge lunge and threw both rocks through the air and into the river.

"Regina," I asked the next week, holding my breath, "would you like to spend the night at my house Friday?"

"Sure," she said. "What would we do?"

"I could take you to see my favorite statue," I suggested.

Regina considered this. "I'm not terribly big on statues," she admitted. "But if we go out at night, we can get some food."

I agreed. "Do you like doughnuts?"

"Do I like *doughnuts*! Be serious!"

"There's this all-night doughnut shop downtown—Flip's—and it's the best place in town. I know you'll love it."

"Great idea," Regina said. "Let's eat doughnuts in the moonlight!" She thought for a moment. "Listen, I'll ask Marge and then call you after supper, okay?"

I nodded. "Why do you call your mother Marge?" I asked.

Regina frowned. "That's her name," she said abruptly.

Regina came over that Friday wearing a dark-blue shift and striped espadrilles, her hair in a sleek, white-blond bun. She looked about twenty years old. My mother and father tried to hide their surprise, but I caught them exchanging raised eyebrows as I pulled Regina into my room and shut the door.

"They think you're the smartest girl in our class," I informed her. "Try to act intelligent."

"Got it," she said.

We watched TV in my room, waiting for my parents to go to bed. At eleven-thirty there was a soft knock on my door.

"Yes?" I asked curtly.

"It's me," my mother announced. She opened the door and stuck her head inside. "I just wanted to make sure you girls are all set for the night. Do you have a pillow, Regina?"

Regina nodded, smiling politely.

"Are you all set?"

"We're fine," I said. "Good night."

"Good night, girls." My mother hesitated, as though she wished she could stay. Then she shook her head, gave us each a little wave, and closed the door.

"She's so *nosy*," I said apologetically. "She just *has* to check on me."

"She seems okay, Arly," Regina said, a little wistfully. "Did you say she's a teacher?"

I nodded. "Anthropology. Boring."

Over our heads we heard the sounds of my parents settling in upstairs.

"We'll wait another half hour," I said. "Then we'll go."

At midnight, I silently lifted my bedroom window and climbed through, dropping to the grass below.

Behind me, Regina stretched her long legs out the window with surprising agility. We tiptoed through the yard and into the alley, then broke into an exhilarated run, both giggling wildly.

"Doughnuts first," Regina insisted. "I'm dying for a double chocolate."

Soon we left Flip's with a bag of the still-warm doughnuts and headed for the north end of the bluff. There were lights from the boats all along the river, and as we drew closer, the black silhouette of Fireman Joseph could be seen against the sky. I approached him at a half run, with Regina beside me. He looked more stark and fierce than I had ever seen him. I felt suddenly scared. Maybe I shouldn't have brought Regina here so soon. Maybe she'd think Fireman Joseph was dumb.

Regina shivered. I couldn't speak.

"*This* is your favorite statue, Arly?" she asked finally.

"Sort of," I answered.

"Why?"

"Oh, I don't know. No big reason."

"You must have a reason. I mean, this isn't your typical park statue, you know."

"Never mind," I mumbled. "Let's just go." I started walking away.

"No, wait," Regina insisted. "Let's eat here. There's something strange about it here that I like." She smiled and pointed up at Fireman Joseph. "He'll be our protector in the night."

31

She folded her legs underneath her on the grass and held out a doughnut. When I sat beside her, she added, "This will be our meeting place. When our mothers are driving us crazy, we can come here and comfort each other. If I say meet you tonight, I mean be right here, under the fireman, okay?"

"After midnight," I agreed, and worry was replaced by a wave of happiness, for at that moment it seemed to me that Regina understood me. We finished our doughnuts and walked along the river until we grew sleepy.

Once back in my room, we slept heavily, through the night and into the morning, until my mother called us for a late breakfast, complaining that we would sleep half the day away.

Five

I had no definite plans to tell Regina about David. He was still too much of a secret, although now I saw him only in the mornings when he boarded the bus to the high school. I had to get up very early to do this, and sometimes now I was tired from meeting Regina at Fireman Joseph's, but it was always worth it. Even a fleeting glimpse of him still thrilled me. And knowing that now I could confide in Regina about other things, like my unhappiness with school and my mother, was enough of a miracle in my life; there was no need to bring David into what was growing between us.

By May I had taken her
to the other, showing h
could think of. We mus
pair—Regina so tall in her sophisticated dresses and
shoes, me in my jeans and oversized T-shirts, listening
avidly to every brash word she uttered, always wanting more.

On weekends, when there was no one to ogle or
judge her, she dressed in jeans like I did and wore her
hair in loose yellow braids. And I, conversely, began
to want more color in my closets and to wonder if I
would ever be able to wear anything, even a pair of
pastel socks, with Regina's authority. My new height
made it necessary to buy summer clothes, and I was
drawn to more dashing colors—purples and oranges.
When I showed these to my mother, she gave a little
nod of approval, although she was hurt that I hadn't
invited her to shop with me.

"I see," she remarked, "that you've decided to look
like a girl this summer."

I tried to be patient with the questions she asked
about Regina's family. I had learned that Regina had
two grown-up sisters, one who lived close by and one
who would soon be home from college for the summer,
but I still hadn't met anyone from her family. And
although we saw each other nearly every day, Regina
had never once invited me into her home.

"So what's Regina's house like?" my mother asked
one Saturday morning while I was waiting for Regina
to come over. "Did you say she lives on Wilcox?"

"Oh, it's a beautiful house, Mom, I said. I couldn't resist adding, "Much nicer than ours."

"Of course it is," she replied huffily. "And I suppose Regina's mother is a lot nicer than yours, too."

"Marge Miller?" I asked. "Have you ever met her?"

She thought for a moment. "I saw her at the PTA a few weeks ago, but I didn't speak to her."

"What's she . . . what did you think of her?"

"She looked like a pleasant person." She paused a moment and then added, "I couldn't help noticing that she didn't look like what I would've expected Regina's mother to look like. Regina must look like her father."

"He lives in California," I said.

"Does he? They're divorced?"

I nodded uncomfortably, knowing that a pile of questions would follow.

"For how long?" she asked, concerned.

"A few years. At least a year. I don't know exactly."

My mother seemed surprised. "Regina hasn't talked about it?" she said.

"She told me he was in California. I didn't want to be nosy," I said defensively.

She nodded, accepting this. "I'm sure you'll have lots of time to talk this summer," she said. Then she asked, "So what does Regina's mother do?"

"Oh, she keeps busy," I said vaguely, embarrassed not to know this either. "With various things. I think she was at one time a teacher." I knew this would please her.

"Really!" she exclaimed. There was a knock on the back door and Regina poked her head inside.

"I'm early," she announced. "But I had to get out of the house." She pushed a strand of hair out of her eyes and bit her lip, her face flushed. She was upset about something.

"Come in and sit down, honey," my mother said in a kindly voice. "Have some lemonade."

Regina sat down and took a deep breath, as though she'd been running. Her hair was falling in damp tendrils out of a single braid.

"You're losing your braid," my mother noted gently. She placed a glass of lemonade and an English muffin on a plate in front of Regina. Regina smiled gratefully up at her.

"This dreadful hair," she said dramatically. "This is the time of year when I just *hate* it."

"Relax a minute and I'll fix it," my mother suggested. She ran for a comb and a glass of water.

Suddenly, I felt terribly annoyed. It had been years since my mother had fussed with my hair. She seemed altogether too eager. And Regina lifted her chin with a little pleased smile, like she was at a salon, while my mother organized strands of hair for a tighter braid.

"Does your mother know how to do this?" my mother asked.

Regina grimaced briefly. "God, no," she said. Then she added, more conversationally, "Sometimes I let my sister Hilda fool with it when she's home from college."

"What's she studying?" my mother asked.

"She doesn't have a major yet," Regina explained. "I think she's interested in physical therapy." She was telling my mother things she hadn't gotten around to telling me yet, and I fidgeted with irritation.

"There you go," my mother announced, finished. "That should help. You look stunning."

Regina gave her head a quick shake. I looked away.

"I have some papers to look over, so I'll leave you two," my mother said magnanimously. But then Regina asked her a question about her anthropology classes, and she dawdled happily. By the time we actually left, I was furious.

"Jesus, Regina!" I blurted as we walked into the yard. "I can't believe how you went on and on with my mother like you're old pals, after all this talk about how our mothers drive us crazy!"

"Your mother is not like my mother," Regina announced gravely. "You don't know how lucky you are to have a mother you can talk to."

"I *can't* talk to her," I reminded Regina. "She interrogates me every chance she gets!" I was exaggerating, too angry to stop. "And why do you keep saying I'm so lucky? What's so terrible about *your* mother?"

Regina put her head down, her face suddenly distraught, but I was too fired up to back off.

"We're supposed to be friends and you never tell me *anything*! Why won't you tell me about—"

Regina lifted her face, and I was surprised to see her eyes brimming with tears. It silenced me. Regina

37

blinked and tears fell down both cheeks, streaking the front of her sweat shirt.

"Regina," I implored softly, "I was only trying to—"

"She's *not* my mother," Regina announced in a low voice. "I don't have a mother. I don't expect you to understand." She wiped her eyes fiercely and glared at me. "Are you satisfied?"

Then she turned and ran from me down the street, and I was too stunned to call her back.

I hoped that Regina would be at Fireman Joseph's that night. I waited in my room for what seemed like days, watching the clock, listening for my parents to go to bed. Finally, at twelve-thirty, I left the house, half running all the way to the north bluff. I sat in the grass, waiting, until to my great relief I heard the swishing sounds of Regina's approaching bicycle. She climbed off the seat without looking at me and sat in the grass, laying her blond, still-braided head on her arms.

"Regina," I entreated softly, *"please* don't be mad at me."

Regina lifted her head. She looked exhausted, and her eyes were red. "Oh, Arly, it's not you," she said. "Your questions just came at a very bad time. I was going to tell you about it anyway. But it's a hard thing for me to talk about."

"We can talk about *anything*," I insisted. "We're *friends*. I know what it's like to have problems with your mother. And Regina," I added soberly, "I'm not the kind of person who would care whether or not you were adopted."

Regina covered her eyes with one hand and gave a little groan. "Oh, Arly," she said, "you just don't understand."

I was silent, waiting for her to explain. She looked at me, took a deep breath and went on. "It's not as simple as just being able to say that I was adopted. Nobody has ever said anything to me about being adopted. And my dad . . ." She shrugged. "He's my real father. But Marge . . ." She stopped and shook her head. "Something isn't *right*. I just know it."

"*What* do you know?" I asked.

"I know I'm not hers. From the bottom of my heart. And so I don't know who I really am."

I couldn't think of anything to say. I put one hand on Regina's shoulder and patted her, hiding my confusion.

"Do you want to hear the worst part?" Regina continued in a ragged whisper. I nodded. "The worst part is how much I *hate* her."

"Oh, Regina—"

"No, I do hate her. I *despise* her. I have for years."

"Please don't say that, Regina. You're just upset about—"

"Arly," Regina said, lifting her wet face, her eyes bright and fierce, "you don't know. Because you're so nice and you have a nice mother. You don't know what it's like to have feelings like this. It's like having a secret every single day of your life."

39

I was still patting Regina's shoulder, feeling useless and shocked.

"Oh, God," she moaned into her arms. "I thought it would help to tell you. But admit it, Arly," she said accusingly, "now you think I'm really sick, don't you?"

"No, Regina," I said, keeping my voice calm. "You're my *friend*. And I'm . . . glad you told me. I thought you weren't telling me anything about your family because you didn't like me enough."

"I just didn't want you to think I was screwed up." Then Regina began to cry again, making small gasping sounds like a child who has been crying for hours. I had never before been alone with anyone who was so upset. It made me feel desperate to find a way to cheer her, to distract her.

"Regina," I began in a hushed voice, "I have something to tell *you*. Since we're telling secrets."

Regina wiped her eyes. "Oh, my God," she said, a hint of irony coming back to her voice. "I hope it has nothing to do with your mother."

"It doesn't," I said. "It's about a boy."

"A boy?" Regina asked. "A boyfriend?"

"A boy I . . . follow. I've been following him around St. Martins for months."

"Since when?" Regina asked. "You're always with me."

"I know. I haven't done much following since we started seeing each other on weekends. Lately I only see him in the mornings before school."

40

"Like a secret admirer?"

"Oh, it's much more than that," I said. "Just thinking about him makes me feel happy and—I don't know—important."

"What's his name?" Regina asked.

"David," I said reverently. "David Dolores. And you're the first person I've *ever* told about him."

Regina took this in, her eyes round and curious.

"I would die," I added in a whisper, "if anyone else knew."

"Oh, you can trust me," Regina said quickly. She looked relieved that I had given her something else to think about, and I was glad I'd told her.

"I do trust you, Regina," I answered. We stood up and hugged each other hard, a badly focused hug because she was taller and we were both exhausted and wobbly kneed. We walked silently together along the dark bluff toward our houses, Regina guiding her bike in the grass between us.

"Regina, will you tell me more about Marge?" I asked.

"I suppose I will," Regina said. "Now that you know how I feel." She looked away from me and sighed. Then she brightened a bit and asked me, "Will you show me your David Dolores?"

This seemed suddenly like a terribly exciting suggestion. "If you want," I said, "I'll show him to you tomorrow. He has a music lesson at three o'clock."

"I'll come by your house then," she said. "At two."

41

Before we parted, she said, "I feel so much better, Arly. It's so good to have someone like you to talk to."

Then she gave me a weary but dazzling smile and pushed off on her bicycle into the night, away from me.

Six

All the way to the edge of the first ravine, Regina kept asking me questions about David. I was walking slightly ahead of her, feeling uneasy, unsure now that showing her David Dolores was the right thing to do. What if it meant nothing to her?

"But why this particular boy, Arly?" she asked from behind me. When I didn't answer, she continued, "I mean, why *him* and not somebody from our class?"

It was impossible to answer questions like these. I grew more and more afraid that Regina wouldn't understand. I quickened my pace ahead of her.

"Arly!" Regina called, unable to keep up with me.

We were almost to the ravine's edge, and I turned to face her.

"Regina, why did you wear those *shoes*?" I asked, pointing to her red clogs. "I don't think you can make it in them."

"Sure I can," Regina insisted. "I'm fine."

"This is a shortcut to his house," I explained, pointing into the ravine. "And if we go around the ravines now, we'll be too late and miss him completely."

Regina frowned thoughtfully. "Well, I *wish* you had said we'd be *climbing*," she complained. "But I'm sure I'll be okay. Lead on." And she started climbing down the incline ahead of me.

She did have a terrible time staying on her feet, slipping, skidding to her knees, clutching at trees for support, but she was laughing at herself, enjoying the adventure. I kept turning around, asking her if she wanted to go back, and she would call, "No *problem*, I'm right behind you!" with her hair in her eyes and her legs splattered with mud. At the top of the third ravine, she leaned against a tree and panted, "Holy God, Arly! This David Dolores had better be something!"

I was too nervous to be amused, afraid we might miss David altogether, but more afraid that Regina wouldn't be impressed. We emerged in silence at the back of the Dolores property, Regina too winded to speak and I too anxious. I led her to the dilapidated garage and she collapsed on the newspaper stack, trying to catch her breath. When I looked out the grimy window to see if we'd made it in time, Regina stood up and peered over my shoulder, squinting.

"He'll be out in a minute," I said soberly. "We made it just in time."

"I can't wait!" Regina whispered. "I'm dying of curiosity!"

She put her head beside mine and rubbed a small circle clear for herself on the glass. After a few minutes, the back door of the Dolores house swung open and David stepped out with his instrument case in one hand and a portfolio under his arm. His back was to us.

"I can't really see him," Regina complained softly.

In that moment, a red-shouldered hawk flew up from the ravine behind us. It circled the yard and then flew up over the garage, out of sight. David turned toward us, following the bird with his great dark eyes. His hair had blown forward, across his narrow forehead, and he was dressed in a white shirt, faded jeans, and an old-fashioned argyle vest. He was facing us, gazing somewhere above where our faces were frozen against the clouded glass.

"Don't even move," I begged Regina in a whisper. "I don't think he can see us."

After what seemed like an eternity, David turned and walked down the narrow sidewalk that ran alongside his house and then disappeared from view.

I let out a deep breath.

"Oh, Regina," I exclaimed, "I felt so trapped. He's never looked back here like that before."

"He was looking at that hawk, wasn't he?" Regina asked.

"He's an ornithologist," I explained.

"A what?"

"A bird-watcher."

"Oh, really?" Regina exclaimed. She was silent for a moment.

"Well, say something, Regina!" I blurted. "What do you think of him?"

Regina smiled at me. "Now I can see why you picked him, Arly," she said. "There's something strange about him, isn't there?"

I nodded. "Don't you think he's incredibly handsome?"

"Oh, absolutely," Regina assured me. "He's unusually handsome. But strange. Like us."

"Oh, Regina," I sighed happily. "For a moment there I was afraid you'd take one look at him and think all of this was silly."

"Nothing you do seems silly to me, Arly," Regina protested. She added cheerfully, "I think your David Dolores is just perfect."

"Isn't he?" I agreed. "Today was like seeing him again for the first time. Come on, Regina. I'll show you where he goes for his oboe lesson."

"Not the ravines again!" Regina cried.

"No, come on. It's sidewalks all the way."

We walked to the warehouse and slipped inside to the stairs beneath the broken window. Regina sat beside me. Soon the rich, somber sound of David's oboe floated into the warehouse. It was the end of his lesson; he was playing the oboe solo from Borodin's *Polovetsian Dances*, which I knew he had worked on all through the spring. That afternoon, he played it so beautifully that I closed my eyes, overcome. When the music stopped, we peeked over the peeling windowsill and watched David leave the house with a formal wave to his teacher inside. His face was solemn, but I could tell by the way he was carrying himself that he was pleased.

"A musician, too," Regina remarked softly. "He sounded just like a professional."

"He's one of the best musicians in the state," I said. "I think he's going to be famous."

Regina's eyes widened; she was impressed. We looked out the window again, but David had disappeared.

"How about if we go and get a hamburger while you tell me about him?" Regina asked. "I'm ravenous!"

"I doubt if he has a girlfriend," I said on our way back downtown. "I think he's too completely devoted to his music."

"Is his family rich?" Regina wondered. "I thought his house looked unusually elegant."

"It's just his mother," I said. "Her name is Althea. She—"

"Just his *mother!*" Regina exclaimed. "He lives *alone* with her?"

I nodded.

"The poor thing," Regina said sympathetically.

47

"Living alone with your mother can be pure hell."

I hadn't given this much thought. Regina was looking off, thinking of something. "What's his mother like, Arly?" she asked abruptly.

I shrugged. "I don't know. I wouldn't even recognize her if I saw her. I don't think the two of them do very much together."

"That's understandable," Regina said. "But I wonder what she's like."

And for the rest of the afternoon she talked about what Althea Dolores might be like—what sort of woman would live on her own in a huge place like the Dolores house, and what sort of mother would have produced a musician-ornithologist like David. I was surprised by this. It occurred to me that Regina had never mentioned a single boy since we'd met. I could understand her not being interested in the noisy, skinny boys in our junior high. But she seemed to me to be the perfect type to have an older boyfriend somewhere, writing her letters and poems. I wondered if this might be another secret she was waiting for the right moment to tell me about.

The next morning we met on the corner near her house. Regina's face was glum.

"Another fight with Marge?" I asked as we fell into step together.

Regina sighed. "It's beyond mere fighting," she said. "Lately it's best for me to avoid her as much as I possibly can. My sister will be home soon from college. I'm hoping that will help." She was silent a moment, then she shook her head, as if to empty it of unhappy thoughts. "Where are we going this morning?" she asked, brightening. "Are we following David again? I'm definitely in the mood."

We headed north. "Regina," I began, "did you know any interesting boys in Minneapolis?"

She gave me a sideways look. "What do you mean, *interesting*?"

I made my expression nonchalant. "Oh, someone who you especially . . . liked?"

Regina looked away. "I didn't have someone I followed around like *this*," she said, her voice somewhat curt. "If that's what you mean."

"That's not what I mean," I said, but wondering now if I should just drop it.

"Well, what *do* you mean? You mean like a *boyfriend*?" She looked unmistakably defensive.

"I just thought you seemed like the type who might have—"

"I prefer to have nothing to do with boys, Arly," she announced.

"I know what you mean," I agreed quickly. "But I was thinking you might have known some . . . *older* boys."

Regina looked at me as we walked. She seemed to be deciding whether or not to tell me something.

"Boys don't like *me* either," she muttered. She looked away.

49

I scrambled for something reassuring to say. "It's just because boys our age are too young and stupid to appreciate—"

"Sometimes I wonder," Regina was saying, "if they can tell that I'm . . . that I'm not . . ." She paused, thinking, and looked back at me. I was listening, waiting.

"You might as well know this, too," she said grimly. "I'm not normal for my age."

I thought she meant her unusual height. "Oh, now, Regina," I insisted, "it's very in to be tall nowadays. Everybody thinks—"

"I wasn't referring to my height," she interrupted impatiently. "I mean, I'm not *normal*."

I looked at her, bewildered.

"I'm not *developing* normally," she said, frowning.

A thought struck me. "Oh, do you mean like having your period and all that?"

Regina sighed.

"You mean your period?" I asked again.

Regina was still looking away, but she nodded.

"You haven't had it yet?"

"Ar-ly!" Regina shouted. "Do I have to spell it out for you?"

"Oh, I get it," I said quietly. I lowered my head, thinking hard. Finally I asked, "Regina, what does that have to do with my question about you having a boyfriend?"

"They know when you're not normal," Regina explained curtly. "Boys, I mean. They can just *tell*." She was suddenly on the verge of tears.

"It must be hard," I said quickly. She nodded, composing herself.

"What does Marge say about it?" I asked. As soon as the words were out of my mouth, I realized they were wrong. Regina grimaced, then stood up, her face flushed with disappointment.

"*Marge!*" she cried, throwing her arms up wildly. "What am I going to say to *her* about it! My God— it's her *fault*, Arly!"

In my confusion, I stopped in my tracks and put my fingers to my temples. "Wait a minute," I said. "I missed something. How can you not having your period be Marge's fault?"

Regina was as frustrated as I was, deeply upset that we weren't communicating.

"I'm sorry, Regina," I said earnestly. "But I honestly don't get it."

"It's her fault," Regina explained loudly, as though I were deaf, "because she won't admit that she's not my mother. I don't know who I really am and it's made me—abnormal."

She had turned very pale. There was a long, wary silence between us, then Regina looked away.

Finally I spoke. "Regina," I said gently, "I think maybe I'd better meet Marge."

"I don't want you to meet her," Regina admitted.

"But Regina—"

"You won't understand. Nobody else ever has."

"I'm your *friend*, Regina, remember? How can you say I won't understand? I want to meet her so that I *can* understand."

Regina gave me a long look. "You'll think she's just fine," she said accusingly. "Like everybody else does."

"Regina—" I began again.

"All right," she interrupted. "Okay. I'll arrange it. I'll tell Marge that you're coming for dinner on Sunday. Both my sisters will be there. You might as well meet them too."

For the rest of the morning, we talked about other things, but what Regina had said stayed with me, troubling me after we parted. I even briefly considered asking my mother about it, and this made me remember my own first period and how she had fussed over me. But if I asked her about Regina, then she would want to know everything. So I kept it all to myself and waited for Sunday.

Seven

"What's the big deal?" my mother asked as I tried to make my hair lie down on my forehead. She took the comb from me, and for once I let her help. "Is this some kind of special occasion at Regina's house?"

"Yes," I explained. "Regina's sisters will be there."

"Regina has two sisters?" she asked.

"Yes. The oldest one lives in Stevensville."

"Really? By herself? She must be quite a bit older than Regina. What does she do there?"

The combination of her questions and her combing began to make me edgy.

"That's fine, Mom," I said, taking back my comb. "I can't stand it anymore."

"Don't you worry," she said, looking at me proudly. "Regina's sisters will think you're the cat's meow."

I hated it when she said corny things like that. I rolled my eyes at her in the mirror.

"Be sure to scowl like that a lot," she said. "That will really impress everyone." She left my room, and I put on one of my new purple blouses, nervously fumbling with the buttons.

Before I left for Regina's, my mother tried once again to flatter me. She pointed my new outfit out to my father, trying to get him to compliment me.

"Look at your daughter, Frank," she said warmly. "Isn't she a knockout today?"

I was about to say something sarcastic, but he gave me a look that said *be nice, be nice* and then mumbled, smiling, "She looks like Arly Weston, which is fine with me."

Approaching Regina's house, I again felt surprised at its simplicity, the gray siding, the plain door, the bare cement porch. I pressed the doorbell and waited, shifting from foot to foot. Regina opened the door and grabbed my hand without a word, pulling me quickly through the living room and up a flight of stairs to her own bedroom. I was craning my neck the whole time, trying to look around.

"Regina, for pete's sake," I cried, "what's the rush?"

She shut her bedroom door and leaned against it. She was dressed in a thin purple shift with black stripes and batwing sleeves—the sort of outfit she used to wear to school. She crossed her arms and hunched nervously.

"Where's Marge and everybody?" I asked.

"They're here, they're here. You'll meet them." She frowned. "I just wanted to warn you. My sisters will probably make some snide remarks about this being the first time you've been here."

"That's all right," I assured her. "I'll act normal about it, don't worry."

Regina flounced onto her bed and started brushing her hair roughly. "So what do you think of my room?" she asked.

I looked around. Regina had a canopy bed with a blue-and-turquoise silk-screened butterfly hanging between the posts. Her walls were painted a deep violet color, and she had a series of art nouveau posters in shades of pink and lavender of women in furs and large-brimmed hats with swirling hair. It was just the sort of room I would have expected Regina to have.

"Oh, Regina," I said admiringly, "I just love it."

Regina smiled, relieved. "This room is my salvation," she said. "The rest of the house is too boring to even look at. So don't expect anything."

I nodded.

"Dinner will be in half an hour," she went on, pulling the brush through her hair.

"It smells good," I said.

Regina made a face. "It's pot roast," she apologized. "Don't get your hopes up."

"Regina," I chided gently, "quit being so negative." I pointed to the closed bedroom door. "I want to *meet* them."

She sniffed and stood up, fluffing at her hair in the mirror. "Okay," she said. "All right. You might as well." She opened the door and led me back down the stairs.

In a recreation room off the kitchen, Regina's sisters were playing cards. Both were small brunettes with round faces and friendly smiles. They were wearing pastel jogging suits, one blue and one yellow.

The sister in the yellow suit was facing us, and she put her cards down when we came in.

"Well, hi!" she said. "So you're Regina's mysterious friend, Arly."

Regina's other sister had turned around. She was smiling, too.

"Arly," Regina announced in a formal voice, "this is my sister Hilda and my oldest sister, Ruth."

Ruth stood up and reached for my hand. She was the smallest of the three, at least a full head shorter than Regina.

"My mother says she was beginning to wonder if you really existed," Ruth said. "Hilda and I are playing cribbage. Would you like to play?" I looked at Regina.

"We have to set the table," she said curtly.

"Well, don't go this *minute*," Hilda admonished. "We're glad to meet you, Arly."

I nodded shyly.

"So, how long have you lived in St. Martins?" Ruth asked me in a friendly voice.

"Arly doesn't appreciate nosiness," Regina announced. I gave her a shocked look, but she had already turned on her heel and left the room.

"Excuse me," I said apologetically, following her. Behind me Hilda laughed. "Those kids and their secrets."

Regina was in the living room. "They're like two old ladies with that damn cribbage," she said, scowling.

"It was all right, Regina," I insisted. "I didn't mind Ruth's question." Regina rolled her eyes.

"Should we set the table?" I suggested. Regina stood up without answering and led me into the kitchen. A small, round-shouldered woman was skimming gravy over the stove. Her hair was brown, like Hilda's and Ruth's, but with streaks of gray over either temple. She was wearing a faded polyester pantsuit. When we came in, she turned.

"Arly," she said in a soft, uncertain voice. She looked much older than my own mother. "I'm sorry I didn't meet you at the door, dear, but my hands were full." Her face was flushed and slightly damp.

"That's all right," I said politely. "Regina showed me her room."

"We'll set the table now, Marge," Regina said. She

began stacking plates noisily from the dish cupboard. Marge winced momentarily at the clatter and then smiled at me.

"We're so happy you could join us for supper," she said. "Regina has told me how you have to work for your father on Sundays."

I looked at Regina. "Yes," I said softly. "But not today."

"Well, it's a treat to finally meet you," Marge added.

"I think she got the message," Regina snapped. Then she sailed out of the kitchen with an armload of dishes.

"I'm very glad to be here, too," I said, embarrassed. I grabbed a stack of plastic cups and left the kitchen quickly. I wanted to beg Regina to stop being so rude, but Hilda and Ruth had joined her in the dining room and were helping her set the table.

"Something smells great, Mom," Hilda called. "Are we about ready?"

"It'll be a little while yet," Marge called back. When Regina heard this, she let out a loud sigh.

"Marge, you *said* half an hour!" she exclaimed.

Marge poked her graying head around the doorframe. "I *know* I did, but I forgot about the beans." Her voice was straining to be patient. "It'll just be a few more minutes, girls."

"Well, we're going upstairs then!" Regina said insistently.

"Stay down here a minute," Ruth protested. "We want to visit with Arly."

"Why don't you girls sit down and talk together in

the rec room?" Marge called. "I'll bring the food to the table myself."

I hurried to the rec room and sat down, avoiding Regina's eyes. Regina followed her sisters with her arms crossed over her chest. She stood pouting for a few minutes and then sat down at the card table beside me.

Hilda and Ruth began to ask me questions about my family, about school, about what St. Martins had been like to grow up in.

"Keep talking, everybody," Ruth instructed, standing up. "I'll give Mom a hand."

Soon Marge called us. She brought a heavy pot roast surrounded by carrots into the dining room and set it at the head of the table. Then she smiled at me over the steaming platter. "I hope you're a meat-and-potatoes lover, Arly. Regina tells me your mother is a gourmet cook." There was an apologetic note to her voice, and I shook my head.

"Not really," I said. "She just buys a lot of gadgets."

Hilda and Ruth laughed.

"Well, you take as much as you want, dear," Marge urged.

"Or as little," Regina added, under her breath. Everyone ignored the remark, but I could feel the tension mounting. I looked up from my plate and caught Marge looking right at me. She gave me an odd smile, as if to say, *Don't be alarmed, this is normal here.* I smiled back uncomfortably.

"The meat is very good," I said. At my elbow Regina

59

was cutting at her meat with her eyebrows knotted.

"My piece is like leather," she said archly.

"Oh good," Hilda said brightly. "Maybe it will get stuck in your throat."

Regina glared, and a tremor went around the table. Marge looked at Hilda warningly.

"Sorry, sorry, sorry," Hilda apologized wryly. "Excuse me for being so *rude*."

She passed me a bowl of potatoes. "Do you play cribbage, Arly?" she asked, her voice pleasant again.

"I am *sure*," Regina exclaimed, "that Arly came over here to play *cribbage*!"

"Look, no one is going to force Arly to play cribbage against her will!" Hilda said.

"It would be all right with me," I insisted, but no one was listening.

"Quit trying to embarrass me!" Regina shrieked at Hilda. "I can't *believe* how much you love to embarrass me!"

"Could we please just eat now, girls?" Marge asked.

"I can't eat this!" Regina cried, pushing her plate away. "I *hate* red meat and nobody gives a damn!"

Ruth had been silent a long time, but at this she stood up, threw her napkin onto the table, and pointed a finger at Regina.

"Just sit down, Ruthie," Marge begged. "It's nothing."

"I will not listen to her insult you, Ma!" Ruth declared. "I don't care who is here. I won't have Arly leave this house thinking we *allow* this creep to talk to you this way. Your mother made this entire meal for you, Regina, you little bitch, so shut up and eat it before you get this pot roast right in your lap!"

"Ruthie, please," Marge implored.

Ruth sat down and picked up her fork. "Everything is *perfect*," she said in ringing tones to her mother.

I was afraid to look at Regina. I was cutting my meat into tiny pieces. Peeking around the table, I saw that only Marge seemed markedly distressed. Regina pressed my knee under the table, and I looked at her then, making my face a question: *Why?*

Regina's blue eyes were flashing—for an instant she looked almost triumphant. She lifted her eyebrows, implicating me in her warfare. *See what I mean?* her expression said. I looked away.

As we finished the meal, Ruth seemed to be making an effort not to look at her youngest sister. She and Hilda pushed away from the table and went into the rec room. Marge began clearing away the dishes with a crestfallen face. Only Regina was self-satisfied.

I got up and followed Marge into the kitchen to thank her for the meal.

"I'm sorry that I have to leave so soon," I said. "But I have to help my father."

Marge seemed surprised that I would thank her. "Oh, you're welcome," she said. Then she gave me the same defeated smile. "Do come back again," she called after me as I left the kitchen.

"You're leaving now?" Regina asked. She looked less sure of herself.

"I promised I wouldn't stay long," I said uneasily. "I'll walk you a little ways," Regina offered, and I nodded. On the street she said urgently, "So you've seen them, Arly. Now you know what I've been talking about all these weeks." It was more of a question than a statement, and when I looked at Regina's face her expression was again almost pleading. "Oh, Arly," she entreated, "do you understand now what I have to go through every day of my *life* in that house?"

Her lower lip was trembling. Looking at her, I remembered that I had promised her that she could count on me.

"It must be very hard, Regina," I said quietly, and once I had said it, Regina's face immediately relaxed into sadness.

"It is. I truly don't know how much longer I can stand it," she said in a thick voice. Then she threw one long arm around my shoulders and hugged me as we walked. "How can I ever thank you for being my friend?" she wondered aloud. And again, before we parted, she called to me, "I'm so glad you understand."

A bank I passed said that it was only four, too early to reappear at my house—my mother and father would still be eating their own Sunday dinner. So I walked farther, to the bluff. At Fireman Joseph's I sat in the grass and rubbed my forehead. I was angry at myself for letting Regina think I had been in league with her against Marge, who seemed to me more of a tragic figure than anything. I would never have treated my own mother that way in front of company, no matter how much she'd annoyed me. I was glad that Ruth had come to Marge's defense.

I looked up at Fireman Joseph, involved as usual in his endless rescue mission, and I groaned.

You're no help at all, I accused him. My head ached. Then I remembered the pleading look on Regina's face as I'd left her house. She was my friend, my only friend, and we needed each other.

Eight

Monday was Memorial Day, and my mother had an uncontrollable attack of curiosity about Regina's family. She followed me back and forth to my room all morning, determined to get answers.

"What did you think of Regina's sisters?" she asked, standing in my doorway. "Are they as pretty as Regina?"

I answered in monosyllables.

"Did they say anything about their father? What do you suppose he's like? What does—"

Suddenly I covered my ears and flopped onto my bed. "Quit asking me so many questions!" I yelled.

She flinched, but held up her chin. "I really don't see why I shouldn't ask my own daughter a few simple questions," she said coldly.

"Mom, I don't want to talk about it now!" I cried. There was an unhappy silence between us, and then my mother's face collapsed. She put her head against the doorframe and started to cry.

"Oh, Mom, *don't*," I began, sitting up, but she turned and left me. From above, I heard the door of her bedroom closing. I fell back onto my bed. How could I have answered her questions? I was still trying to sort out my impressions. I lay in a discouraged heap until the clock on the wall reminded me that it was time to get ready to meet Regina. My gym shoes were under my bed, and I put them on listlessly. When I looked up, my father was standing in the doorway.

"Your mother is crying," he announced. "What is the matter with you?"

I was silent a moment. Then I said, "She was asking me too many questions again."

"She didn't use to *have* to ask you questions," he insisted, "because you used to take the trouble to talk to her once in a while. You know, Arleena, I'm beginning to think this independence thing is going a little too far."

"I need my privacy, Dad," I said, but without conviction.

My father frowned and shook his head. "Arleena, your mother has a perfect right to ask you how you are spending your afternoons." His voice was rising.

"You have plenty of privacy. And I would appreciate seeing just a little more understanding and *courtesy* from you. Is that clear?"

When he was gone, I covered my face. He was so rarely angry at me. I left the house quietly, dragging myself through the streets, clumsy with remorse.

At Fireman Joseph's, Regina was lying on her back in the sun. I expected to find her equally depressed after yesterday, but she sat up when she heard me and gave me a cheerful grin. From the grass she lifted one long leg, shaking her foot at me. She was wearing red, high-top sneakers.

"Get a load of these, Arly!" she called. "Especially for climbing through ravines!"

I plunked down beside her without answering.

"Arly, what's wrong?" she asked.

"I had a fight with my mom this morning," I said. "Even my dad is mad at me."

Regina scoffed. "Really, Arly," she said. "I'm *sure* it's nothing. After that scene at my house yesterday, I would think you'd see how lucky you are to have *normal* parents."

"If you're so *unlucky*," I snapped, "then what are you in such a good mood about today?"

Regina thought a moment. "To tell you the truth, Arly," she said, "I've been feeling so relieved that you finally got to see how bad things can be at *my* house. Now you won't think I get upset over nothing."

Before I could say anything, Regina stood up and jumped up and down in her new shoes.

"Come on," she urged. "Let's cheer up. I'm ready to do some serious stalking."

We hurried through the ravines to David's. I didn't know what he would be doing for the holiday, but I was sure we'd see him sooner or later if we were patient. Regina and I took turns watching, both anxious to be distracted by the sight of him. We waited for almost half an hour; then during Regina's turn, I heard her gasp.

"Someone's coming out," she whispered. "Oh, my God, Arly. It's the *mother!*"

I had never seen Althea Dolores before, and I stood beside Regina at the window and watched Althea leave, mildly curious. I was surprised to notice that she looked so very young—too young to have a son as old as David. She was wearing a gauzy blouse and a tiered skirt with leather sandals. Over one thin shoulder she carried a leather bag. Her dark hair was pulled back to the nape of her neck in a thick bun. We watched her walk up the narrow sidewalk beside her house and away from us before we could see her face.

"She didn't take her car," Regina whispered. "She's walking. Let's go!"

"Wait a minute," I protested. "Go where?"

"We're following her. This is our chance to find out what *she's* like."

"I don't care what she's like!" I exclaimed. "I want to wait for David."

"Well, then wait," Regina retorted. "I'm going to follow his mother." She hurried out of the garage

67

without looking back. I caught up with her, grumbling, but she paid no attention. We circled the block and hurried down Langley. When Althea's small figure came into view ahead of us, Regina slowed.

"Why are we doing this?" I complained. "She's probably not going anyplace interesting."

"*Look* at her, Arly," Regina said. "She looks so elegant and important, like somebody famous. Can you imagine having a mother who looks like that? Oh, I wish she'd turn around."

At the corner of Langley and Main, just south of downtown, she did turn, at a light, glancing over one shoulder before crossing the street. I saw then that she had David's piercing, dark eyes and straight eyebrows. She was very beautiful.

"Jesus, look how she walks," Regina commented softly. "The same way your David walks." She pulled my arm, hurrying me, and we crossed the street together. It was odd to have Regina leading, but her fascination was contagious.

Althea Dolores walked south along the bluff for nearly a mile while we trailed her. Then she came to a path that led to the lake. She paused for a moment at the top of this path before she disappeared. We hurried to the same spot, crouched at the top of the bluff and looked down, just in time to catch sight of her walking farther south, along the water's edge, winding her way over the rocks and around the rusted breakwaters.

"Hurry!" Regina cried, descending the side of the bluff.

I jumped after her. When we reached the bottom, Althea was gone. We figured she was still heading south, her path hidden by overgrown shrubs and cottonwoods. So we continued. On our right the water grew more rough and noisy. Gulls soared above our heads, crying plaintively.

Regina and I walked side by side, through the flash of spray.

"She must be close ahead," Regina said, and I nodded. We came to a wall of short, twisted cottonwoods and quickly circled them, moving away from the water.

Just beyond, to our shock, sat Althea Dolores on a spread blanket, attaching a lens to her camera. She saw us the same instant we saw her and gave a little gasp.

"For heaven's sake," she exclaimed. "You two startled me!"

We both stood looking at her, our mouths open. I couldn't believe we'd made such a blunder. I elbowed Regina desperately, prodding her to say something.

"Um . . . we're lost," Regina stated unconvincingly.

"Oh, you are *not!*" Althea protested in an amused voice. "Nobody gets lost walking along the beach." She put her camera down and shaded her eyes, looking us over.

"We didn't mean to disturb your . . . photographs," I offered nervously. "We'll be going now." I pulled Regina's arm.

Regina ignored my tugs. "Were you photographing

69

those boats?" she asked, pointing to the sails on the horizon.

"No," Althea said. "I was photographing the gulls." We looked out over the water, to where three white gulls were gliding over the waves. "They're not usually found on the Great Lakes. Those are Icelandic gulls." She smiled again, and the dark line of her eyebrows softened. She had taken off her shoes and unfastened her hair. There were tiny streaks of gray in the strands along the sides of her lovely face.

"Did we scare them off?" I asked apologetically.

Althea nodded. "They'll be back. So what are you two girls doing in this no-man's-land?" Her voice was full of approval. "I never see anyone else out here."

"Oh, we come here all the time," Regina lied. "We love bird-watching on this part of the beach."

I tugged at her arm again. "We have to be going," I announced for both of us.

Althea nodded pleasantly and picked up her camera. "Enjoy your walk, girls," she said.

"Thank you," Regina called over her shoulder. After a few more steps, she added, "Enjoy the Iceland gulls."

"Icelandic," I muttered beside her.

"God, she's incredible!" Regina exclaimed as we headed back up the beach.

"That was so *embarrassing*!" I cried.

"It was *not*," Regina argued. "She was *glad* to see us. In another minute she probably would have asked us to sit down with her."

70

"Well, I never would have—spying on her and then practically falling right on top of her blanket. *God*, Regina!"

But Regina was smiling to herself. She said softly, "She was so *nice* to us. It felt like something out of a movie. Oh, Arly, it was meant to happen. I can't wait to see her again."

Her face was glowing as she said this. I was suddenly glad that we had done something together that had made her so happy.

"It *was* fun," I admitted.

"God, I feel good," Regina crowed. "It's going to be such a *wonderful* summer!"

Nine

It was the final week of school. Regina's newfound optimism for the summer ahead was contagious; we were both filled with energy. I imagined weeks of roaming, eating lunch on the river, riding our bikes, and, of course, watching David together. But Regina insisted that we go back to the spot where we had seen Althea. We went every afternoon of the last week of school, but we never saw her there again. I grew impatient. We hadn't seen David in almost two weeks.

"Regina," I said, as we climbed the bluff for what seemed like the hundredth time, "doesn't it feel like we're just wasting our time coming down here like this?"

"Yes," Regina agreed, unexpectedly. "I was just thinking the same thing, Arly. I have a better plan. You'll like it, I promise. It has your David in it."

"What plan?" I asked suspiciously.

"Just listen. I'll spend the night at your house tonight, and we'll go to David Dolores' house real late and spy through their front window and—"

"Regina!" I cried in alarm. "People get arrested for that!"

"Please don't be silly, Arly. Nobody will arrest us, because nobody will *see* us. We'll be *careful*. And it's the only way to find out what they're truly like."

"I can't do that," I pleaded. "I *can't*."

"For heaven's sake, Arly, you look like a scared rabbit!" Regina exclaimed. "This isn't such a big deal. We *have* to do it! You're the one who got me started with all this following business, you know."

"You can't blame this idea on me," I protested. "And I can't do it."

"*Please*, Arly," Regina said, pulling on my arm. "If you won't come with me, then I'll have to do it alone. I'm so curious about Althea Dolores that I can't endure it another day. Oh, please, Arly, don't make me do it alone."

I stared at her, shaking my head. What really upset me was that Regina actually *would* go to that house without me. I couldn't bear the thought of missing whatever she might see there. I shut my eyes and groaned, feeling caught.

"But Regina," I pleaded, "what if we end up getting into *trouble*?"

"We won't, we won't," Regina cried. "I'm absolutely positive. It will be *fascinating*—I just know it— I can feel it in my *bones*."

I groaned again, but finally agreed to go. All the way back to my house, I worried about it. I knew it was reckless—and irreversible. I walked into my living room wringing my hands. My mother was reading on the couch and she looked up at me, waiting for me to say something. She and I had a wary sort of truce since our last fight.

"Listen, I was wondering, Mom," I said, trying not to sound upset. "Could Regina sleep over tonight?"

"I guess that would be fine," she agreed quietly. "But weren't you just with Regina at *her* house?"

"No."

"You weren't with Regina?"

"I wasn't at the Millers'."

"Where were you then?"

"Out," I said, an old reflex. "Walking."

"Oh yes, I *know*. Walking." She sighed and lowered her gaze to the book in her lap. "Do whatever you want," she said, without looking up.

Regina decided we would leave my house early that night—it was only ten o'clock when we slipped through the back door and set out in the rain. I knew my mother would look for us before she went to bed, but I didn't care if she discovered us gone. Maybe I secretly wanted her to put a stop to what was happening.

"Oh, your mother knows we go out for walks when we feel like it," Regina reminded me as we slipped through my yard. "She won't think anything of it."

"She will too," I disagreed. "Not that you *care*."

Regina was wearing a navy-blue rain parka; ahead of me she made a dark wet silhouette. I slouched along several yards behind her.

"You're supposed to be the adventure lover," Regina chided me over her shoulder. Then she stopped, waiting for me to catch up. Her face was shiny with rain, but radiant. "Come on, Arly, get in the spirit of this."

But I felt so wrong about the whole thing. The rain had already soaked though my thin jacket; I felt bedraggled and lowly.

Regina decided that we shouldn't take the ravine route because it would be too muddy. So we walked on the sidewalk, not even trying to hide.

"Let's go back," I pleaded, a last-ditch effort. "Let's do this when it isn't raining."

"Arly, this rain is perfect!" Regina cried, flapping her arms like a huge bird. "It will make us harder to see!"

She was walking so fast that we were in sight of the Dolores house in less than fifteen minutes. There were lights on in the front windows. Between us and the windows was the room-sized pillared porch.

"I'm not going up on that porch," I whispered. "Someone from the street could see us."

Regina pointed to a smaller porch on the side of the house with three steps leading up to it—a separate entrance. She headed toward it and I followed. By now my heart was pounding, but Regina seemed unafraid. She pulled my arm and I climbed the three steps. We stood on either side of the small glass pane in the top half of the door, hidden in shadows. I could hear music from within; I recognized the Winter movement from Vivaldi's *Four Seasons*—one of my father's favorites. I was shivering wildly.

"I'm not going to do it," I whispered, more to myself than to Regina. "I won't look in."

But then Regina, ignoring me, put her eyes to the corner of the glass and peered inside. She squinted and gave a deep sigh of satisfaction. And I couldn't bear not knowing what she was seeing. I took a deep breath, leaned against the door and lifted my eyes to the glass.

I will never forget the scene within. Facing us, in the dimly lit living room was David, his entire glorious length stretched out on an antique sofa. His hair was tousled; he was dressed in a T-shirt and running shorts, his legs white as bones and his long feet bare. If he had been completely naked, I couldn't have been any more astonished at the sight of him. Off to one side, Althea was curled in a reclining chair. She wore a loose, summery gown that covered her legs; her feet were under her. Her hair was falling out of a topknot, curling around the sides of her face. They were both listening to the music; one speaker was at David's head. His eyes were closed and he was smiling. Althea was watching him, smiling, too. It was a scene of such tenderness and intimacy, and I felt suddenly so fiercely wrong to be watching them, that I was filled with panic. I turned away and grabbed at Regina's arm, pulling it roughly.

"Let go of me," she whispered. "What's the matter with you?"

"It's wrong. It's illegal and wrong. Let's leave— Regina, please, please, I beg you—"

"Jesus, calm down, Arly," she said, hushing me. "I just want to get one more look at her and then we'll go."

But I gave her arm such a final yank of protest that she stumbled and swayed momentarily at the side of the porch and then fell backward, her mouth a silent O of alarm, onto the grass. I was horrified at the muffled noise of her fall. I climbed down and huddled beside her, praying no one would come to the door. The music reached a crescendo inside.

"I'm hurt," Regina moaned beside me. "I twisted my ankle."

"Get up," I whispered fiercely. "Don't just sit there, get *up*, Regina."

"I'm *hurt*," Regina repeated. "It's my damn ankle!"

Somehow I knew what she was going to say next. I closed my eyes in dread.

"I need help, Arly," Regina said. "Go and get her."

"I *won't*," I announced in a low voice. "I don't believe you. I'm going home."

"Please," Regina entreated. "Just ask her to help me. She'll recognize us."

"Oh, God," I cried. "Are you completely crazy? We could get in really big trouble!"

"Please," Regina begged. "Just ask her. I can't get up—I swear I can't. If you want to leave, leave, but get her for me before you go."

"I'm getting the hell out of here," I said, and I started to scurry away. But when I looked back at Regina, huddled beside the porch steps with one hand on her ankle and her head bare, I was shocked at how desperate she looked, her eyes wet and pleading in the light from the streetlamp. I gave a little moan of anguish, ran back up to the side porch past her, climbed the stairs, and gave that door a series of crashing blows to break through the music. Then, without a word to Regina, I ran away, crying like a lost child all the way back to my house.

When I stumbled into the kitchen, my mother was making bread.

"Arleena!" she cried. "I thought you were in your room!"

"I went for a walk," I mumbled.

"A *walk*! What *is* this? It's almost eleven o'clock! You didn't even tell me you were leaving!"

"You said I should do whatever I want," I reminded

her. She was about to explode angrily, when she looked more closely at my blotchy face. "Honey, are you crying?"

I nodded miserably, while a puddle formed at my feet. "Mom, I'm freezing," I moaned. "Could you please get me a towel?"

"Arly, where's Regina?" my mother asked, remembering our plans. I followed her into the bathroom, my head aching.

"She got sick," I said. Then I shook my head and started again. "She didn't get sick. We had a fight."

She was filling the tub with hot water, adjusting the temperature, and she looked up at me. I sat on the hamper and pulled off my soaked tennis shoes, my eyes welling with tears again.

"Oh, honey," she said. "I'm so sorry. Do you want to talk about it?"

"I'm too upset," I said, wiping my face with a towel. How I wished there was a way to tell her what had happened. But there was too much to explain—where would I begin?

"Well, take your bath then. You might have caught a chill. We'll talk in the morning."

I nodded gratefully, and she hugged me and left me alone. But even in the tub I couldn't get warm, and I shivered for the next hour, until she and my father put me to bed with the heating pad and extra blankets.

Ten

The next day I woke with a terrible head cold and a sore throat, made worse by guilt. It was the middle of June, a hot clear day, but I lay in my bedroom, shivering. My mother brought me water and aspirin, and my father came in with a concerned face and set up the vaporizer at my bedside.

"People are not supposed to get colds in June," he admonished gently.

Later my mother came back to the side of my bed. "You have a visitor," she announced softly. "Are you up to it?"

"Oh, no!" Regina said when she saw me. "Oh, poor

Arly!" She sat down on the side of my bed.

I was angry, but achingly curious. I sat up and scowled at her.

"Well?" I urged. "Go ahead. Tell me what happened."

"I'm so sorry you're sick, Arly," Regina said earnestly. "I feel like it's my fault—"

"It *is* your fault," I agreed. "Just tell me what happened."

"First tell me you're not angry," she begged. Then she added, "Oh, I don't blame you, if you are."

"You were just using me last night," I accused. "You just wanted to see Althea. I should never have come."

"I know, Arly," Regina admitted. "But I couldn't help it. I got carried away. I just had this feeling that last night was the night that was going to change everything. And once I looked at her inside that beautiful house, I just had to meet her, really *meet* her. There was nothing in the world I needed more." Regina hugged her knees. "Please try to understand," she said.

"Well, I *don't* understand," I grumbled. "I don't see why we had to do such a crazy thing."

"Arly, it's all *right*," Regina insisted, leaning forward. "It's all right. Althea understands." She sounded as if Althea were an old friend.

"God, Regina," I said in alarm. "What did you *tell* her?"

"Oh, now, don't worry," she soothed. "Althea doesn't know about you and David. I just told her that I had been wanting so badly to meet her and that I had come over, but I fell down on her steps because they were so slippery. I told her that you were my friend, but that coming to her house was my idea. So that you wouldn't be embarrassed."

"I *am* embarrassed!" I cried. "And you've ruined everything. How will I ever be able to even *look* at David again?"

"You can not only look at him, Arly, you can *meet* him. You can meet them *both*. Althea invited us over tomorrow."

I sank back onto my pillow. "Oh, no, I could never face them," I groaned. "I just can't believe you've done this."

"Arly, please believe me. Everything is *all right*. Althea *likes* me. And David wouldn't know you from Adam."

"Did you meet him?" I interrupted. "Did you talk to him?"

"Only a little," Regina said. "I was talking with Althea."

The thought that Regina had actually been in the same room with David Dolores made me suddenly dizzy. I covered my face, wanting to cry out in distress.

"Come and meet her tomorrow," Regina urged. "You won't believe how nice she is—I talked to her for almost two hours. She even gave me a ride back home."

"Regina," my mother interrupted from my doorway, "I think Arleena needs to rest. Why don't you

82

say good-bye and plan to see her tomorrow or Monday?"

"Tomorrow?" Regina asked me, and I nodded uncertainly.

"I see your ankle healed quickly," I said resentfully as she was leaving.

Regina looked guilty, but then smiled a dreamy, generous smile. "Arly, I *am* sorry about last night," she said softly. "And I'm sorry that you're sick, too. But you'll see tomorrow that it was all worth it. *Trust me.*"

After she left, my mother checked the vaporizer and put a cool hand against my forehead. "Don't get your hopes up about tomorrow, honey," she advised. "You might be out of commission a little longer than that."

I sighed. My throat was beginning to ache terribly.

"Did you make up with Regina?"

"Oh, sort of," I croaked. "It's a long story, Mom. I'll tell you about it when my throat stops hurting."

"Your father and I would like that," she said gently, but firmly, and then left me alone to sleep.

Regina called the next morning, but in the night I had taken a turn for the worse. My mother told her this on the phone. Although it was a relief to have an excuse not to go back to the Dolores house, I couldn't help feeling left out. I tossed and turned in my bed all afternoon, unable to rest, too sick to get up.

My mother came in carrying a tray of soup. "For

83

God's sake, Arleena," she exclaimed. "Just lie back and *rest*!"

My father stuck his head into my room. "That was Regina on the phone again. She said for me to tell you she had a marvelous day. Or did she say magnificent? Or majestic? She said she'd tell you all about it tomorrow."

I frowned and pushed my soup away roughly.

"What *is* it, Arleena?" my mother demanded then. "Why are you so upset about all of this? Your father and I are worried. What happened with you and Regina last weekend?"

I looked from her face to my father's. I wanted suddenly to tell them—at least some of it.

"All right," I said. "But let me tell it my own way."

They both waited for me to begin. "Regina has met this woman," I said. "An older woman. Her name is . . ."

"An older woman?" my mother interrupted. "What do you mean Regina has met an older—"

"Mother!" I cried. "Let me *tell* it! An older woman named Althea Dolores and she lives on Langley. Regina thinks this woman is the greatest person who ever lived, and she wants me to go to her house with her and meet her too, but I . . . but I . . ." I was floundering, and my mother jumped back in.

"Please, honey," she pleaded. "Tell me where Regina met this—"

"I know Althea Dolores," my father interrupted. "I know her, Helen. She's the widow with the boy who's so talented on the oboe." He looked back at me curiously, making an earlier connection.

"But what would this woman want with Regina?" my mother asked.

"Regina thinks she's the most amazing person she's ever met," I repeated grudgingly. "I guess she's an artist or something."

My mother turned to my father. "Does this sound all right to you, Frank?"

"I'm sure it's fine, Helen. Althea Dolores is a regular customer of mine. She's a very talented photographer. She and David moved here from the East Coast after her husband died. Apparently she grew up near here. David—the boy—is a musician. Brilliant, according to Ed. And I can certainly see why a girl like Regina would be impressed with Althea Dolores. She's not your usual St. Martins housewife."

Then my mother gave me a thoroughly puzzled look. "But I don't understand what this has to do with why you and Regina were fighting Saturday night. Didn't *you* want to meet Althea Dolores?"

I sighed. "Well, for one thing, Mom, I don't understand why Regina is so mean to her *own* mother. It's like she *hates* her, and now she's so impressed with Althea Dolores, but I just can't see—"

"Wait a minute, Arly. Back up. Regina hates her own mother?"

"She even says that Marge isn't her real mother, Mom."

"She does?"

I nodded. My mother paused, not wanting to push, then asked, "Is it possible that she's right?"

I shrugged. "Well, Regina doesn't have any proof. She says it's just something she feels inside."

"Oh, I see." My mother paused again. "And does this have something to do with why you two were fighting?"

I lowered my head. "That was something else. The main thing was that Regina wanted me to meet Althea, but I didn't want to. I didn't feel right about it."

"I don't see why you *have* to, if you don't want to," my mother said. "After all, Regina's friends don't all have to be your friends."

This was no comfort at all. I fidgeted. "Well," I said finally, "I wouldn't feel right about *not* meeting Althea either."

Both my parents looked confused.

"I just don't understand what's so terrible about Marge," I went on. Then I looked away from them and added silently: *And why did it have to be my David's house and my David's mother?*

They both knew that I was leaving things out. But this was the most I had confided in either of them in months. My mother stood up and patted my leg.

"I know you two girls can work it out," she said. "Let me know if there's any way I can help."

"Don't get discouraged, Arly," my father added. "All friends have their disagreements."

I nodded. There was still so much they didn't know

that I almost called them back. But I decided not to; I wanted to try and face Regina myself.

Regina came by the next afternoon. I was glad to see her, but I didn't show it. She was looking more bright-eyed and glowing than ever.

"You missed a wonderful time," she announced, "but don't worry. When I told Althea that you were sick, she said we would do it again, just as soon as you're better. What about Thursday? Will you be well by Thursday?"

I lowered my eyes, hesitating.

"David is out of town, Arly. At a music camp. So he won't be there at all."

"He's gone?" I asked. I felt both relief and a pang of loss. "He wasn't there?"

"Yesterday, he was. But he's leaving today. While I was there he mostly listened to records in his room. He didn't say anything to me."

I was glad to hear this. "How was it with Althea?" I asked.

"Oh, it was heavenly!" Regina exclaimed. "I mean, she is the most utterly fascinating woman! She's a professional photographer *and* a painter *and* she has this fabulous quilt collection! Wait till you see her studio—you won't believe it!"

She leaned forward on my bed, her eyes shining. "Arly, she is just as wonderful as I knew she would be from the first time I saw her. And on top of everything, she really likes me! Yesterday, she said to me: 'I can tell that you're unusually well traveled for your age.' She called me 'well traveled,' isn't that wonderful? She said she would be happy to show me how to use watercolors, if I was interested. Oh, Arly, she's like a dream. I can't wait for you to meet her, too!"

I was overwhelmed. "Well," I said softly, "maybe I could come with you Thursday. If you're sure David won't be there."

"Oh, he's gone. I'm sure. Although, truthfully, Arly, I don't see what the big deal is. He doesn't know anything about our following him."

"It's not just that, Regina!" I began, but Regina wasn't listening. She had already stood up and was planning her next move.

"Can I use your phone?" she asked. "I'll call Althea right now and see what time we should come on Thursday."

In a few moments she bounded back into my room and jumped onto the foot of my bed. "She's invited us for lunch! Can you stand it?"

"I hope so," I said.

"Why don't you meet me there, at her house?"

"No!" I cried. I couldn't stand the thought of walking up to that house alone. "Let's meet at your house."

"Why on earth would you want to come to *my* house?" Regina wondered. "You'll have to talk to Hilda and Marge."

"I'll be there at noon," I said firmly.

*   *   *

88

When I knocked on Regina's front door the next day, Hilda let me in. She was dressed in jeans with her hair in curlers, eating a carrot.

"What's up, Doc," she said and then laughed at her own joke. "Come on in, nice to see you."

"You, too," I said shyly. "Where's Regina?"

"She's still in the shower," Hilda said. "She said to tell you to go straight up to her room and wait. You know, don't hang around us too much, you might die of boredom."

"I'm not bored," I protested. "I'll just stay down here and wait."

Marge came out of the kitchen in a ruffled apron. I was again struck by how much older she looked than my own mother.

"Well, well," she said pleasantly. "How are you?"

"I'm fine," I replied. "I'm not sick anymore."

"Oh, were you sick?" Marge asked. She looked briefly confused. "I didn't know . . ."

Just then Regina came roaring through the room with her head in a towel. She grabbed my arm as she passed me.

"We'll be down in a minute," she cried and pulled me up the stairs to her room.

"Arly, listen," she announced, shaking out her long hair into the towel. "Marge doesn't know about Althea. She thinks I've been hanging around with you all week. Don't blow it!"

"I won't," I said. "But I think you should probably tell her the truth."

"*Tell* her?" Regina exclaimed. "Come *on*, Arly! You know yourself there're some things you can't explain to your mother!"

I did know this, but somehow I felt that Marge's ignorance of Althea was unfair. Still, I kept quiet about it.

"We're late," I pointed out mildly.

"Oh, it doesn't matter," Regina assured me. "Althea's very loose about schedules." Her eyes lit up suddenly. "She's making lunch for us, Arly! I'm sure it will be something fabulous! Oh, just wait until you see that beautiful house! You'll faint!"

I didn't faint, but it was easy to see, as we stepped into Althea's house, why Regina was so impressed. Althea led us into the large high-ceilinged living room, the room I had first glimpsed through the side porch window. Most of the furniture was antique, and the white walls were hung with quilts and abstract paintings. There were odd decorative touches everywhere, an old ceramic piggy bank on a dresser top, a row of antique dolls on a bookshelf, handmade mobiles in the doorways. On one wall was a large framed photograph of a man standing against a backdrop of spray and breakers, a tall, stately-looking man with a face like David's, but craggier, older. I stared at it until Regina's voice broke the spell and I turned to be introduced to Althea.

"You remember Arly Weston," Regina said. "From the beach?"

Althea smiled warmly. "Of course I do," she said, extending a thin hand. She was dressed in a loosely woven red cotton shift, and around her neck was a string of tiny ceramic birds. She wore flat white moccasins and her legs were bare. Her only makeup was a spot of color on either cheek and a rose crescent over each eye. She looked stunning. I felt suddenly terribly shy.

Althea's kitchen was pleasantly cluttered with pottery, tea jars, and tin boxes. A large window overlooked her tiled sink with a view of the bird feeders and rosebushes. Althea lifted a bamboo tray of teacups and led Regina and me back to the living room. On the way I glimpsed another photograph of David's father, this time seated on a horse, holding a small, round-eyed boy of four or five against his lap.

"Althea, I *love* your beads," Regina gushed.

"These?" Althea said. "Yes, they're nice, aren't they? David brought them back for me when the band went to Mexico."

At the mention of David's name, I dropped my eyes and blushed furiously.

"Arly has never seen David," Regina announced, to put me at ease, but the falsity of it made me feel worse. I coughed and scrunched down onto one end of the antique sofa.

"Well, you'll meet him sometime," Althea said mildly, settling into a chair across from us and handing us our teacups. "But right now he's at Interlochen.

So I'm very pleased to have guests. The house has been feeling rather empty."

"Could I show Arly your studio?" Regina asked eagerly. "I've told her all about it."

"Of course," Althea said. "You girls go on up yourselves and I'll finish my sauce."

We climbed the circular oak staircase, then walked through a long hallway with bedrooms on either side. One room was obviously David's; the door was ajar and my eyes fell on his checkered bedspread. There was a black silk kimono over one bedpost. I gasped and looked away. At the hallway's end there were three framed photographs of David's father with Althea; in one frame Althea lay in a four-poster bed with a baby asleep in her arms.

We climbed another short flight, which led to the third story and a huge attic room. The room to the studio was shut, and tacked to it were recent photographs of David in his backyard, stretched out on a lawn chair, squinting playfully at the camera, his chest bare. Binoculars hung beneath a triangle of dark hair. I gasped again, and Regina laughed.

"I can't help it," I whispered. "It makes me feel so strange."

"Don't be nervous," Regina admonished. "No one will ever suspect a thing. Least of all David."

"Just hearing his name makes me feel so uncomfortable! Whenever I hear it, I can't help blushing!"

"You'd better just get used to it," Regina said.

I shook my head.

"Get ready for the studio," Regina announced. She gave the door a push and pulled me inside, then opened her arms and did a little ecstatic spin. "Can you believe your eyes?"

She showed me around as though she'd spent months, years in that studio and knew everything there was to know about it, pointing out canvases, albums, photographs, watercolors. The studio had a gable, with a drawing table beneath it.

"I'm going to work here," Regina announced proudly.

Over another drafting table was a bulletin board with row upon row of bird photographs. Althea's quilts were kept in a couple of cedar chests off to one corner of the room. Regina opened them for me and unfolded some of the prettiest. She had already chosen her favorites, her favorite watercolor, her favorite bird, her favorite corner of the studio.

"See?" Regina asked me in a hushed voice. "I wasn't exaggerating, was I?"

Althea's cheese soufflé wasn't nearly as good as my mother's. But if Althea had served Regina a plate of beans she would have raved about it. Althea laughed at Regina's praise.

"Oh, come on, Regina, it's *nothing*," she insisted. "Such a fuss over a soufflé!" But I could tell she was pleased to have us there.

"We're just trying to get on your good side, Althea," Regina teased. "Arly and I eat like this every day!" She rolled her eyes at me. I just nodded, feeling somewhat left out of the banter. It was clear that something important had taken root between them. Althea turned to me.

"Regina has told me that you're quite an expert on out-of-the-way places in St. Martins, Arly," she said warmly. "Have you always lived here?"

I answered several more questions, charmed by her attention. For the rest of the meal I felt better. At the meal's end, Althea brought out a small glazed white cake.

"Taste it," she said to Regina. "It's a little surprise for you." Then she turned to me and winked, as though I would know what it was.

Regina tasted it. "Coconut!" she exclaimed. "I don't believe it!"

"You said it was your favorite," Althea said. "So I thought we should have it today."

Regina savored her piece, cooing and rolling her eyes. Again, I felt jealous, but I smiled at Althea as she handed me my slice of cake.

After I ate it, and Althea had taken our plates to the kitchen, I looked at Regina and said, "I didn't know you were so madly in love with coconut."

Regina giggled happily.

When we left Althea's house, soon afterward, Althea hugged Regina's shoulders fondly and then, a bit more formally, mine.

"Come back and see me, you two," she said. "You don't know how nice it is for me to have met you. And next time," she added to Regina, "we'll do this when your mother isn't working. I'd love to meet her too."

I looked at Regina, but she was walking away from Althea's porch with her head high, almost prancing.

"You told Althea your mother works?" I asked.

"Marge doesn't belong in Althea's house," Regina said shortly. "She wouldn't understand."

"I think she should know. You could tell her," I said for the second time that day.

"Why?" Regina asked. "Your mother doesn't know about David. Marge doesn't know about Althea. It isn't a big deal."

"It's not the same," I insisted softly.

"Well, if Marge can have her secrets," Regina said softly, "then I can have mine. She's *not* my mother, Arly," she reminded me soberly.

Hearing her say this again made me angry. How could she be so sure? And Marge's ignorance of Althea seemed all the more hazardous after I had seen Regina and Althea together.

"Well, I really think you should just tell Marge about—"

"Oh, *sure*. So she could screw everything up and embarrass me?" Regina protested.

"Maybe she wouldn't—"

"Arly, she *would*! Believe me, I know. And *why* are we talking about Marge?" Regina snapped. Then her expression softened. "Arly, we've just spent the most wonderful afternoon of the summer with Althea Dolores. We should be in ecstasy! Didn't I tell you it would be incredible? And can you believe how much she seems to like me?"

"She does," I admitted grudgingly.

"I feel so happy when I'm with her," Regina said. "She makes it seem like life is so interesting and there's so much to look forward to. Isn't she just absolutely *inspiring*, Arly? You saw it, too, didn't you? I'm so glad you were there today. Having you there made it even more special."

I nodded, hiding my doubts. *At least,* I thought, *I'm not in the dark like Marge is. At least I'm still included.*

Eleven

Althea was teaching Regina to use watercolors, and so Regina, who had never before been interested in art, was suddenly filled to the brim with ambition for painting. They both still included me in their unfolding friendship, but I often felt lonely. Sometimes I missed my old solitary treks through St. Martins. Still, it was pointless to complain about this to Regina. She, at least, had found what she'd been looking for.

"Sometimes I'd like to go somewhere *besides* Althea's, you know," I grumbled to her on our way to the studio.

"Oh, Arly," Regina said, "you know how important

this is to me. Besides, I went wherever you wanted to go in the spring."

"*You* wanted to, too," I reminded her, hurt. But we were close to Althea's house, and Regina wasn't really listening.

The next morning we were walking to Althea's when Regina announced quietly, "Oh, by the way, Arly, David's going to be there today. Althea was expecting him to get in last night from band camp."

I froze in my tracks. "Regina!" I cried. "Why didn't you tell me *sooner*?"

"I thought I'd already mentioned it. Besides, you knew you were going to see him eventually."

This was only partly true. For the last two weeks, I had been pretending David and Althea were completely separate phenomena.

"I can't just walk into that house now!" I protested. "You *know* that!"

Regina sighed and gave a guilty shrug. "All right, all right, Arly. I thought it might be better not to give you a lot of time to worry about it. I was afraid you'd panic."

"What will I say? I can't just say: Hello, it's nice to meet you—"

"Why not? It will be nice. He might even really *like* you!"

"You just should have told me sooner!" I cried. "I'm not mentally prepared! I can't do it today!"

"But, Arly, Althea's expecting us for brunch—"

"Then *you* go." I said coldly. "I'm going home."

Regina nodded. She looked only mildly disappointed. It occurred to me that it no longer mattered to her very much whether or not I went along. I bit my lip, fighting tears. "All right, Arly," Regina said. "I'll just tell Althea you're busy."

But as I turned, she grabbed my hand. "Arly, don't go away mad," she implored. "I honestly just didn't want you to worry. Say you'll come with me tomorrow."

"Well, all right," I said, relieved that she still cared. "It's just that you should have told me."

When she went on ahead, I watched her walk away, half skipping, swinging her arms, her whole body in a sort of headlong charge up Langley Street. My anger came back as she disappeared from view. She didn't really care about what David meant to me. She hadn't told me he was there because she didn't want to be inconvenienced. I walked home in a rage, feeling betrayed.

When I got to my room I flung myself on the bed, imagining the moment when Althea would introduce me to David. I knew that if he gave me an even remotely quizzical look, as though he'd seen me before, I would die. And yet I couldn't bear the thought of being left out, of letting Regina see him without me.

"Arleena," my mother called, "could you come here for a minute?" She was reading on the sofa, and I sat beside her. When she pulled a few leaves from the ravines out of my hair, I flinched but didn't get up.

"Listen, honey," she said in a serious voice. "There's something I need to talk to you about. Marge Miller called about an hour ago, looking for Regina. She thought you girls were here. I told her that you'd been invited to another brunch at your new friend's." She stopped and gave me a long, concerned look.

"She didn't know what you were talking about, did she?" I asked.

"She sure didn't. And I didn't know what to tell her either, so it was a very uncomfortable conversation. I did tell her that you girls had met an older woman and were going to her house occasionally—"

"Mom!" I cried in alarm.

"I had to tell her *that*, Arleena."

I nodded soberly, secretly glad that someone had told Marge. "What else did you say?" I asked.

"Well, Marge seemed somewhat concerned, so I did tell her that your father knows Althea Dolores and that I was sure she was a respectable person and that you girls had enjoyed meeting a local artist. But I could still tell that Marge was quite upset that she didn't know anything about it from Regina."

I nodded again. "Regina doesn't want to tell her," I admitted. "I know she should have said *something*, but she doesn't listen to me anymore, Mom. And if I make a big deal about it, she'll probably accuse me of not being her friend."

"Regina should have listened to you, Arly," my mother said firmly. "I'm sorry I had to be the one to tell Marge, but I do feel she has a right to know."

That evening Regina called me. She sounded bewildered. "Why on earth did you tell your *mother*?" she asked. "I didn't know you were telling her any of this."

"I've told her a *few* things," I said defensively.

"Well, now she's told Marge some story about us hanging around at this artist's house and Marge is all upset because *I* didn't tell her."

"That's not my mom's fault," I insisted. "You're the one who said my mom seemed like a person we could talk to. How was she supposed to know it was a big secret?"

Regina was silent. Then she accused me softly, "You're supposed to understand why I haven't told Marge. Why do you sound so angry about it all of a sudden?"

"I just don't think it's my mom's fault," I repeated. "I think you should have told Marge yourself."

Another silence. Then Regina gave a deep, disappointed sigh.

I broke the silence between us. "So is it okay, or what, Regina?" I asked. "You're not grounded or anything, are you?"

Regina laughed mirthlessly. "I'd like to see her try to do something like that to me now," she said. "Oh, don't worry. I talked my way out of it. I told Marge that it was all your idea and that I just hadn't gotten around to mentioning it."

"*My* idea!" I cried. "I can't believe you would tell her that! None of this is my idea!"

101

"I *know* that, Arly. You don't have to shout! It's just something I told *Marge*."

There was a silence between us. "You shouldn't tell *anybody* that," I insisted softly.

"Arly, it's no problem. Don't give it another thought. Listen, did I tell you what a great time I had at Althea's today?"

"That's a big surprise," I grumbled.

"Have you decided to go ahead and meet David? Can you come tomorrow?"

"I think so," I said.

"Wonderful!" she exclaimed. "I just know it will be all right, Arly. Wait till you see your David. He's all tan and thin from camp, and he won some important music award. Althea was so proud of him! She's such a fantastic mother, isn't she?"

"Don't say any more," I pleaded. "I don't want to chicken out."

After I hung up, I went back to my room with an empty cardboard box and sat on the floor beside my bed. Slowly I pulled out all the things I'd collected, lingering over the schedules, the pictures, an article on the band from the newspaper, David's magazines, bird-watchers' books, sheet music. I arranged everything carefully in the box and then pushed it toward the back of my closet. It seemed the thing to do. But I had a sinking feeling.

My dad came to my door to say good night, and I jumped at the sound of his voice.

"What are you so edgy about?" he asked mildly. "Is anything bothering you?"

"No, Dad," I said. "I'm just tired." He left and I groaned softly. My life seemed cluttered with secrets.

My parents didn't know about David, Althea didn't know about Marge, Marge didn't know how Regina felt about Althea, Althea didn't know how I felt about David, and no one really knew how difficult it would be for me to meet him. *How much longer can we do this?* I wondered. I went to bed and fell into a hot, restless sleep.

When it came time to go to Althea's, I dressed in the most drab, inconspicuous outfit I could find, as if I were trying to become invisible. During the entire walk to Langley, Regina chatted to distract me, for I was in a daze, moving forward mechanically with my teeth clenched. Regina kept patting my shoulders encouragingly, telling me little jokes, smiling sweetly. She didn't even complain about what my mother had done the day before. Suddenly we were at Althea's. I climbed the porch stairs with my eyes straight ahead, sweat running down my sides under my gray T-shirt.

"Maybe you could try to look just a *little* more normal," Regina coached patiently. "You're walking like a zombie."

I groaned. Regina pushed open Althea's screen door and called inside, "Althea! It's us. Can we come in?"

"Come in, girls. Put some water on for tea, why

don't you, Regina?" Althea's voice came down from her studio. "I'll be down in a minute."

Regina pulled me along behind her and held my hand while she put Althea's copper kettle on the stove. For the first time since I'd first been in that house, there was a spread of dishes left on the table, the traces of a huge breakfast. When Althea came down, dressed in a white skirt and blouse, she glanced around at the table and smiled, shaking her head.

"Excuse the mess," she apologized. "Da-vid. Please come down and clean up your dishes!"

I felt the blood draining out of my head, and through a roaring in my ears, I heard footsteps on the stairs and a shuffling through the living room. Then, in the doorway to the kitchen, David appeared, his coloring more intense than I had ever seen it, his hair longer, almost to his shoulders, dressed in a plaid pajama top and faded jeans. He was dazzling.

"As much as I love having you home, David," Althea said in a teasing voice, "I'm not about to start cleaning up after you like they do at your rich-kids' camp."

David was about to retort when he looked across the kitchen at Regina and me. His eyebrows raised slightly, registering surprise. I lowered my head, wishing I could disappear.

"Regina has brought her friend Arly this morning," Althea said pleasantly. "Arly, this is my son, David."

"Hi," David said with a nod, and he began clearing up his dishes. I kept my eyes lowered and tried to breathe normally. Regina sensed that I was overwhelmed and reached again for my hand.

"You're busy in here," she said to Althea. "We'll wait up in the studio."

She pulled me along past them and through the living room. "That wasn't so bad," she whispered to me.

"I'm a wreck," I moaned.

"You were fine," Regina soothed.

"Go ahead up to the studio," I whispered. I was burning hot and my heart was pounding. "I need to catch my breath out on the porch." Regina nodded understandingly and went up alone.

I stood outside for a moment, my eyes closed, taking in deep, steadying breaths and leaning for support against the front of the house. From within, through the window screen beside me, I could hear David and Althea still talking softly in the kitchen. David had a deep, melodic voice.

"Another one of your adoptees?" he asked Althea. "Are you starting a home for runaway girls?"

"Oh, be nice about it," Althea chided gently. "I like those two. They're really sweet girls. Regina reminds me a little of myself when I was her age."

"She hangs on your every word and you love it. God, Mom, I go away for three weeks and when I come back you've taken on—"

"I haven't taken on anyone, David. Regina is interested in learning how to paint. The house wasn't quite as empty as it usually is when you're gone. I liked that. Don't be so territorial. No one will bother you."

Then I heard them moving into the living room together, and, afraid of being found on the porch, I moved noiselessly to the railing, climbed over it and ran away from the house up Langley Street. I needed to calm myself and think about what had just happened. I remembered the sight of David, clearing away his dishes in his pajama top. Why had I felt so overcome? And I thought of the conversation between David and Althea. David had sounded almost jealous of Regina and me. This also disturbed me, but at the same time seemed terribly stirring. He had *seen* me, not just Regina, but *me*—I was real to him. He had said hello to me politely, and then later asked his mother what I was doing there.

Then suddenly I remembered Regina, in the studio, waiting for me.

"So where on earth did you go, Arly?" Regina asked me that evening. She had stopped by after dinner and we were in my bedroom. "I even went outside and looked for you in that decrepit old garage."

"What did you tell Althea?" I asked fretfully. "Did she notice how nervous I was to see David?"

"I think so. But I told her you're just a little shy around boys."

I groaned. "Regina, I don't know if I could ever get used to seeing David right in his own house like that," I said.

Regina shrugged. "He left right after you did, Arly. He's in his own world, I'm telling you—"

"Not as much as you think," I disagreed. "He noticed us. I heard him ask Althea about us when I was on the porch. He asked her if we were teenage runaways. Kidding her about it."

"He *did*?" Regina asked. "What did Althea say?"

"She said she liked us." I added grudgingly, "Especially you."

"She said that?" Regina asked, pleased. "Did she say anything else about me?"

"No," I replied. "But she told David not to be bothered about us being there."

"Good for her!" Regina said emphatically. "It's none of his business."

"It's *his* house," I reminded her. I wanted to defend David. "It's his mother, too," I couldn't help adding softly.

Regina's eyes widened. "What's that supposed to mean?" she demanded, her voice rising.

"Oh, nothing," I said, backing down. "It's just that I think it's normal for David to wonder why we're hanging around his house."

"I am *not* hanging around!" Regina objected. "Althea is teaching me how to paint. I assumed you understood the importance of that!"

"I do understand," I insisted. "But I don't think you should act like David isn't important, too."

"I know he's important to you," Regina said. "But I don't think he should interfere with Althea's interest in *me*."

We faced each other angrily, until I looked away.

"Oh, Arly, let's not fight," Regina said. She waited until I looked back at her and then took one of my hands. "I don't want to fight," she repeated.

"Neither do I," I said glumly.

"We have too much to feel good about to be fighting," Regina said, her voice softening. "I'm so grateful to you for helping me to find Althea. Maybe sometimes I get a little carried away about it, but you understand, don't you?"

I didn't answer, but Regina went on. "And I just know it will get easier for you, seeing David and all. You have the entire rest of the summer to get to know him. We have so much to look forward to together."

She went on and on like this until it was time for her to go home. Then she left me in my room, feeling frustrated.

I found my father and mother in the kitchen, sipping wine together, making an elaborate lamb stew.

"Did you hear Regina and me arguing?" I asked.

"Did we!" my father exclaimed. "Regina has a voice like a bullhorn when she gets excited." My mother gave him a stern look.

"We've been arguing more often lately," I said.

"About Althea Dolores?" my mother asked.

"Not just her," I said, but I stopped myself from going on and looked away.

"Arleena?"

"I don't think Regina really cares about our friendship anymore," I reported unhappily. "Now that all she thinks about is Althea."

"I wouldn't be so sure about that, honey," my mother said, disagreeing. "She still seems to want you for a friend. Why else would she come over and call you like she does?"

"She just wants to talk about what she did at Althea's," I complained. "And she never listens to what I think. Unless I completely agree with her."

"Regina has always seemed to me to be the type who overreacts a bit. Let her try and work this thing out with Althea. It's obviously very important to her," said my mother.

"Think about finding a new interest for a week or two, Arly," my father added. "Give her some room. Wait it out."

They were both watching me. I nodded, and yet I knew that there was nothing else in my life big enough to distract me from the drama that was unfolding at the Dolores house. I went back to my room, knowing that I would be walking to Althea's with Regina the next day. I was caught, swept along, and Regina was still in charge.

Twelve

I let a few more weeks pass this way. Regina and I
would walk to Althea's in the late morning, and she
would make tea for us in her high-ceilinged sunlit
kitchen before Regina's painting lesson would begin.
Regina was as dreamy and contented as ever and I
didn't want to fight with her, so I resigned myself to
following her up to the studio after tea, watching her
set up her color charts and exercises and still lifes;
but more and more often, I left her to her work and
wandered home or back to the riverbank, or to the
bluff, alone.

Regina was wrong about me getting used to the

sight of David. Even a glimpse of his belongings—a novel, music left out on his music stand in the living room, a shirt thrown over the back of a chair—seeing those things unnerved me. I had never expected to come so close—to get next to his life. Sitting in his living room and his kitchen, I was always guilty and disoriented, but never enough to just stay away.

Several times during those last two weeks of July, David would be home practicing when Regina and I arrived, although he always left soon afterward to visit a friend named Todd. The first time he said hello to me, and called me by my name, I nearly died. Going over it in my mind afterward, I realized that he had said hello to *me*, and not to Regina. And during the next few days, I noticed that in his reserved and somewhat formal way, he was actually rather nice to me, certainly friendlier than he was to Regina, whom he largely ignored.

Once when Regina had wandered up to the studio and I was getting ready to drift back downtown, I didn't know that David had quietly set up his music in the living room. He watched me coming down the stairs from the studio and caught my melancholy expression.

"You could take painting lessons, too, you know," he said kindly.

"I'm not interested in painting, actually," I replied in a low voice. I forced myself to continue, my color rising. "I'm more interested in . . . music."

"Oh, good for you," David said. "Besides, I've noticed that the studio isn't big enough for anyone else once your friend is up there."

"No," I said. Then, amazed at my own courage, I added, "There's barely enough room for your mother."

He laughed and I laughed, as though we made jokes like this all the time. Then I walked home in a fog of self-congratulatory bliss.

The next day he came silently into the living room and caught me gazing reverently at his oboe. When I realized he had come in behind me, I blushed, but managed to keep from bolting.

He'd been working in the yard, and his chest was bare, his shoulders and arms tanned to an olive color. He was mopping his forehead with a towel, and he smiled at me. I quickly looked from his chest back to his oboe.

"What instrument are you interested in, Arly?" he asked.

Again I struggled to keep my voice normal. "I'm going to start on the oboe next year," I said. "I love the way it sounds."

"*Do* you?" David asked. "I think I was about your age when I started. Are you about thirteen?"

I nodded, enormously flattered that he would have given any thought to my age.

"I played the piano first," David went on, "but once I picked up the oboe, I never wanted to play anything else."

"My dad already has one for me," I told him, overcoming my shyness. "He's the owner of Frank's Music Store."

"Is *that* your dad?" David asked. "I know him! He's even fixed this thing a few times for me!"

I smiled proudly, thrilled to have found more common ground.

"Moth-er!" he called up the stairs. Althea appeared on the landing. "Hey, Mother, did you know that Arly's dad is Frank Weston from the music store?"

Althea came halfway down the stairs. "No, I didn't make the connection, Arly," she exclaimed. "Your dad is such a lovely man."

"I call him Frank-in-Fog because he always seems to be lost in his own little world at the store," David added.

Althea frowned at him for saying this in front of me, but I wasn't the least offended—it was true. Althea called for a tea break, and although David stayed in the living room making reeds, for the first time I felt that I belonged there.

When I left with Regina, walking through the living room behind her, I glanced his way shyly, wondering if I dared to say good-bye. He was just getting ready to play, and he put his oboe down and gave me a brief, comradely wave.

"Say hello to your dad," he called.

Regina noticed. "At least he speaks to you, Arly," she commented. "He doesn't give me the time of day. I think he's terribly conceited. Just because he's a musician doesn't make him *God*!"

113

But I just smiled to myself. She was wrong—he wasn't conceited. I decided to take him the old oboe my father had brought home for me and ask him what he thought of it.

That night I imagined that I had become a superb oboe player in a remarkably short time and David and I were playing a duet together on a concert stage. The audience gave us ovation after ovation, and David gave me roses and beamed at me proudly, amazed at my talent.

I came late to Althea's the next day, so that I could leave the oboe on the porch without having to explain to Regina why I'd brought it. She and Althea were already in the kitchen—I could hear them laughing and talking. When I came in, Althea greeted me warmly and Regina poured me a cup of tea. Althea disappeared to retrieve something from the studio, and just after she left us, David stuck his head through the back door abruptly, already speaking to Althea, obviously expecting to find her in the kitchen. When his glance fell on Regina, pouring more water into the teapot at the stove, he gave a brief, unfriendly sigh of frustration, then said quickly, to cover up, "I saw your head in the window and I thought it was my mother."

"Althea is in the studio," Regina told him in a chilly voice. "She'll be back down in a minute. She's *busy.*"

David caught her tone and stood looking at her a long moment. Then he said under his breath, but audibly, "She's not so busy. She has time to do her baby-sitting."

Regina gave him a terribly insulted look, then turned her back to him and finished making the tea. David walked back out the door without looking at me and into the yard. The screen door slammed behind him. I was horrified.

"Why did you say that to him like that?" I cried.

"Arly, Althea knows he's rude to me," Regina informed me matter-of-factly. "She told me to just ignore it."

"That's not ignoring it! That was more rude than he's ever been to you!"

Regina sniffed at me and shook her head. She put a cup of tea on a tray and carried it up to Althea. I listened to the self-righteous clatter of her shoes on the stairs and made a silent, furious face at her. Through the window over the sink I saw that David had begun to prune the overgrown rosebushes, his dark eyebrows knitted together angrily. I walked out to him. He didn't look at me until I was standing right beside him.

"David," I said, using his name for the first time, "you have to excuse Regina. Sometimes she can sound like a real know-it-all."

He looked up at me, and the stormy expression on his face softened. "She's a real pain," he agreed. He snapped a few more branches for emphasis, the tips zinging into the air around us.

"I think it's because she's a little jealous of you," I

said. David stopped his pruning and looked back at me curiously, waiting for me to go on. "Because you have a mother like Althea. And Regina has a way of taking over when she likes someone."

David nodded, thinking about this. "You know what really bothers me most about it?" he asked me. I shook my head. "I think that my mother really *likes* it. She *likes* the way Regina has practically moved in. They're both just pretending that we can all be one happy family."

"I know," I agreed. I was thrilled that we were having a serious discussion. "I've even tried to tell Regina that. She doesn't listen."

"I can believe that. How is it that you two got to be friends, anyway?" David asked. "You're a lot different from her."

I didn't know how to answer. "She wasn't like this," I said, growing uncomfortable, "before . . . we started . . ." My voice trailed off. David was watching me.

"We were best friends," I finished, shrugging sadly.

"I think I know what you mean," David said quietly. "I know how it is when friendships change. Well, don't worry, Arly, you're welcome here, especially if you're an oboe lover." He gave me an encouraging smile.

"David," I asked, "when you're finished out here, could you come in and take a look at the oboe my dad brought home for me?"

"You brought it with you?" David asked, pleased.

"Sure, I'll be finished in about ten minutes."

I waited for him on the sofa with the oboe in my lap. When he came in, he had put on a T-shirt and washed his hands. He sat on the couch beside me and took the oboe, his arms brushing mine.

"Arly, this is a Chauvet," he said approvingly. "It's old, but it's a fine instrument."

He put it to his mouth and played a few bars of an unfamiliar melody, slightly jazzy; the sound of it gave me chills.

"Oh, this is a fine oboe for a beginner," David went on. "It's a student model—fewer keys. Can you play anything on it yet?"

"Oh, *no*," I said quickly.

"Don't worry. I won't ask you to play. I practiced in my room for a year before I'd even play for my mother."

He laid it back into my lap and watched me settle it into the case.

"You handle it like it's already important," he said.

"It *is*."

"Makes me remember what it was like for me when I started." He smiled to himself a moment, then stood up. "Now I have some things to do," he said. Before he left the room he added, "That remark I made about baby-sitting. To your friend. No offense meant for you, Arly. It's just that she gets on my nerves sometimes."

"Yes, I know," I replied, with only a small twinge of disloyalty. "Mine, too."

Thirteen

"Arly, you'll never believe what happened last night!" Regina exclaimed, her voice wobbly with distress. She pulled me away from my breakfast and rushed us both back into my room. She closed the door and then turned to me, holding the sides of her head with both hands. "Marge went over to *Althea's*!"

"Oh, Regina," I cried. "Were you there?"

Regina shook her head, her eyes wild. "Thank God, no! I was home in my room. I didn't know anything about it until Althea called me this morning and told me!" She sat down on the edge of my bed and then jumped back up again.

118

"Arly, I think Althea was terribly shocked, just terribly shocked to see her. On the phone she sounded really upset with me." She sat back down again, and her eyes filled with tears. "Oh, I hate Marge for this, I *hate* her for this!" she said, her teeth clenched.

"Why do you think she went over last night?" I asked quietly.

Regina grabbed her forehead. "Oh, it was my own stupid fault!" she cried. "I told Marge that I had finally gotten my period last week, and Arly, she just went berserk because I hadn't told her sooner. I was at Althea's at the time that it happened and Althea helped me with everything—I mean, it just wasn't *necessary* to tell Marge, you know?"

My mouth fell open at this news. "*Last* week," I managed to say. "Last week you got your *period*?"

Regina nodded and looked away, wiping her eyes. "I was going to tell you, but I've been so busy—"

"Oh, don't start," I protested.

"Well, I *was* going to tell you, Arly, no matter what you think."

Suddenly I could picture Marge, alone, knocking grimly on Althea's door. I closed my eyes to erase the image; it was too sad. Then I looked back at Regina and remembered the lies she had been telling Althea—the always-working mother, too busy to care what Regina was doing.

"Althea knows now that you never told Marge anything, doesn't she?" I asked.

Regina nodded. "She *called* me," she repeated in a quavering voice.

"Did she sound mad?" This was somehow hard for me to imagine.

"No, not mad. Surprised. *Upset* with me." Regina's voice rose to a sort of shriek at the gravity of this statement.

"Are you going over there now?"

Regina nodded. Then another thought struck me. *Oh, no,* I thought, *what if Regina can't go to Althea's anymore? What about me and David?*

Regina was waiting for me to say something.

"I'll get my shoes," I said quietly, and soon afterward we left my house.

Althea let us in, her face concerned, sad.

"Come in, girls," she said soberly. We followed her into the kitchen and silently watched her lay cups and saucers on the table. She looked as though she were searching for a way to begin. I wondered suddenly if it was more difficult for her because I was there. I looked at Regina. Her face was stormy, unreadable. I wandered to the back door and looked out into the yard. David was there, spraying something over the roses, a bandanna over his mouth. He saw me in the doorway and gestured for me to come over.

"I'll be back in a minute," I said over my shoulder, and hurried out.

David pulled the bandanna around his neck and walked with me farther back into the yard. He ran his hand through his dark hair, making it stand up a little. He hadn't shaved, and the shadow of a mustache made him look unusually rugged.

"Is Regina in there?" he asked.

I nodded solemnly.

"You should have been here last night," he said. "Her mother came over, out of the blue."

"I know. I heard. Was it terrible?"

David thought for a moment. "Not what you would call terrible," he said. "I mean, there was no actual fighting or yelling. It was just very awkward for my mother. She had been thinking all this time that Regina's mother wasn't *interested* in meeting her. It was just very ... awkward. I think they both knew there had been a misunderstanding, but neither of them was quite sure what it *was*."

"It was Regina," I said flatly.

David nodded, then sighed. "I tried to tell her not to be so blind about it. She wouldn't listen to me. She really *likes* Regina. She wanted ... I don't know exactly what she wanted, but I was right. Things weren't as simple as they seemed."

"They're talking about it now."

"Why didn't Regina ever tell her mother about coming over here and the painting lessons and everything?"

I shook my head. "I don't think she tells her anything she doesn't absolutely have to. She hates her."

He seemed surprised. "Really? She didn't seem so bad to me. What little I saw of her."

I nodded. "I don't understand it either. But David, do you think Althea will still be able to give Regina painting lessons?"

"I guess that's what they're settling now."

"I think Regina would die if she had to stop coming here," I said.

David took this in and then shook his head. "But maybe it would be best," he said. "Until Regina straightens things out for herself."

I watched his face as he said this and could see that this was what he hoped would happen—that Regina would step away from his world. Didn't he understand that I would have to stay away, too? Hadn't our conversations meant anything to him? I looked around the yard, then lowered my head, unable to speak.

"What do you think, Arly?" David asked. "Don't you think it'd be better if Regina quit acting like she lived here?"

I shrugged listlessly. "I'd better go back inside," I said.

"Wait a minute, then. I'll come with you."

But the kitchen was empty. We heard voices from overhead and followed them up. In the studio, Regina was back at work on an elaborate still life, and Althea was sorting through negatives. Regina looked like she'd been crying, but her face was pink and relieved as she took up her task. Behind me, David looked into the studio and then, without a word, went to his own room and shut the door.

"I'm leaving now," I told them.

"I'll come down with you," Regina said, putting her brush aside.

"See you soon, Althea," I said at the door.

"Good-bye," Althea called. I saw her give the back of Regina's head a long, troubled look.

"We talked it all out," Regina said at the door in a breathless voice. "I explained my—situation. I told her just how bad it really is. She understands now why I didn't tell her about Marge. Everything's going to be all right—I'm so relieved." She took a deep breath and sighed. "Let's have lunch here tomorrow, Arly. You and me and Althea."

"Marge probably won't want you to," I said, but Regina shook her head.

"I'll work it out," she said. "Don't worry, no one will get upset—it'll be fine."

And I agreed to come, but lingered a moment on the porch, listening to Regina climbing the stairs back up to the studio. From David's room, I heard a loud, discordant jazz record. I shook my head. *You're dreaming if you think this storm has blown over,* I told Regina silently.

Fourteen

I was up half the night, thinking about David. I pictured him coming to my house, just appearing at my door, taking me for a long drive in his car along the beach and the river. I told him I would always love him. He said he loved me too. We embraced and clung to each other.

I imagined countless ways of telling him the way I felt about him—on a long walk to the bluff, in his overgrown yard full of birds and roses, or alone with him on the antique sofa, surrounded by exquisite music.

But when I finally fell asleep, I dreamed I was looking for him, as I had in the spring, but he was gone and I knew I would never see him again. By morning, I was desperate to see him. I waited in my room until ten-thirty, then left early for Althea's. But I was still uneasy about entering her house alone, so I sat on the porch steps to wait for Regina. Behind me, I could hear David and Althea's voices inside the house. They were arguing, and I stiffened as the pitch of their voices climbed. Althea sounded close to tears. I wanted to run away, but I was afraid of being caught eavesdropping and I crouched low.

"It *is* true!" David shouted. "If I say *anything*, Mom, you accuse me of being selfish or antisocial, or whatever you want to call it. Christ, her own *mother* was here, asking you what the hell this is all about!"

"Regina's mother had a right to be concerned," Althea cried. "But you're my son, David. You have no right to object. This is my house!"

"It used to be mine, too, until you decided that she's more important than I am!"

"David, that's not *true!*"

"Isn't it? Isn't it? Well, I apologize! Maybe I should apologize for being just your son instead of someone like Regina who follows you around this house like a servant, treating you like some kind of *goddess!*"

There was a terrible silence. I sat cringing against the front of the house. "Oh, David," Althea said tearfully, "is that really how all of this seems to you?"

Then I could hear the sounds of him storming up the stairs to his room. I waited until I heard Althea go back into the kitchen and then I climbed down from the porch as noiselessly as I could and hurried away.

All afternoon I worried about them. I walked to the river and back and wandered around downtown, asking myself over and over how I had let such a thing happen. I remembered the first night I had seen them through their window, as elegant and peaceful as a dream. And now they were fighting about Regina—and *I* had led her into their lives. And yet neither of them was thinking of me at all! David was obviously concerned only with Regina and his mother. The emptiness I'd felt with him in the rose garden came back full force, and I felt robbed. He'd forgotten I existed.

Regina! I thought miserably, clenching my fists. Regina had done this to David and Althea—and to me. She had usurped my fantasy with her own, and worse, she didn't care how much hers was costing everyone.

I stood at the edge of the ravine in a rage and yelled her name, my voice disappearing into the trees and brambles. But what would I do without her? She had taken over my world. I was afraid to be alone in it again.

My mother was holding the phone when I came in. "It's Regina," she said softly. "She's called twice today already."

"I won't talk to her," I announced, and sailed into my room.

During supper, Regina called again. "Tell her I'm

126

not having supper here, Mom, please!" I begged.

She frowned, but I heard her say into the phone, "I'll be sure to have her call you tomorrow." Then she came back to the table. "I don't like having to lie for you, Arly, and Regina sounded upset to me. Now what's going on between you two?" she asked.

"I don't want to talk to her," I insisted. Then I added, "I'm giving her some *room*. Like you and Dad suggested."

"But, Arleena, Regina has a right to know if you've decided not to see her. She deserves an explanation, after all."

"I can't get her to listen to me anyway, Mom," I said darkly. "She never really did."

"Oh, now, honey," my mother objected. "I hate to hear you sounding so pessimistic."

"I *feel* pessimistic," I said. "I can't stand it anymore."

"Well, it's not the end of the world, Arleena," she soothed, patting my shoulder. "And I'm sure you'll have other friends as soon as the school year starts."

Hearing this made me want to scream. She didn't understand how complicated and treacherous the whole business of having friends was for someone like me. I had been friendless an entire year before I met Regina. The thought of going back to school to face another void made me run from the table and collapse onto my bed.

The phone rang again, and I heard my mother get up to answer it.

127

"If it's her, tell her I've gone to bed," I cried, pulling a blanket up to my chin. "It's the truth."

The next evening, there was a knock on our front door. My mother and father had gone out for a walk, and I thought it was them, returning. When I opened the door, to my surprise, I found Regina's sister Hilda. She looked as though she had been running, her hair damp and frizzy and her forehead wet.

"Hi, Arly," she said. "I was hoping this was the right house. Is Regina here?"

"No," I said. "I haven't seen her in a few days."

She was panting, and I pointed to an easy chair near the door. "Come in and sit down."

"Thanks. I'm just a little winded—I rode Regina's bike." She sat down to catch her breath. "This is serious business," she began bluntly. "You wouldn't say Regina wasn't here if she was, would you?"

"*No*," I insisted. "I honestly haven't seen her. Has she been gone all day?"

Hilda nodded. "She was gone before breakfast. She and Mom had a talk yesterday that sort of blew her mind. She hasn't been here at all?"

I shook my head. "She's probably at Althea Dolores'."

Hilda groaned. "I was afraid of that. I sure wish I'd found her here instead."

"Why, what's happened? Did Regina and your mom have a fight last night?"

"I wouldn't call it just another fight," Hilda said

128

grimly. "I'd call it a battle royal. My mom told Regina she's decided to move back to Minneapolis. We still have a house there."

"Oh, *no*," I exclaimed softly.

"Oh, yes. Things have gotten so bad between them that Mom has to do something. Regina doesn't even speak to her anymore, unless you count the insults. I mean, I can't *believe* the abuse Mom's had to put up with this summer. Then finding out about Althea Dolores was just the last straw."

"But why does your mother want to move away?" I asked, stunned.

Hilda shrugged. "It was better between them in Minneapolis. Regina was happier, she had a good school, some teachers she liked—she wasn't half as mean to Mom. I guess Mom wants to try and get back to that. At least improve things a little."

I nodded. "But Hilda," I said, "Regina won't want to leave."

"Hah!" Hilda exclaimed. "No kidding! You should have heard her last night. You'd think we were sending her to Siberia! She had us up half the night with her carrying on!"

Hilda shook her head ruefully. "I know she doesn't want to move again. But, my God, if you could hear the things she says to her own mother. I would never dream of talking that way to my worst enemy!" She paused and sighed wearily. "I don't blame Mom for deciding to do this," she said. "She's getting pretty desperate. I even hate to go back to school and leave her alone with Regina. It kills me to see her treated this way."

I was taking all of this in numbly, and Hilda stood up then, shaking her head. "Look, I'm sorry for going on and on about this to you, Arly," she said. "I know you're Regina's friend, and I don't mean to make her sound like a monster."

"You don't," I said. "I know about her and ... Marge."

"Do you know that she says to Mom, right to her face, that she isn't her real mother? I mean, can you top that?"

"I've never been able to understand it," I said softly. After a moment I added, "I'm pretty sure Regina is at Althea's. She must still be awfully upset."

"Well, my mother's gonna be just as upset when she finds out that's where Regina went," Hilda announced. "She told her not to go there today. I was hoping we could avoid any more confrontations. But it looks like I'd better get back and tell Mom. She'll want to go over there herself, I'm sure." Hilda sighed. "What a mess that girl has made of everything.

"Good-bye!" she called to me, walking back to the bike. She pedaled away, mumbling to herself and shaking her head.

I began to pace back and forth in the living room, wondering what to do.

By the time my parents returned, I was beside myself.

"Mom! Dad!" I cried. "Regina's sister Hilda was

just here. She told me that Marge has decided to move back to Minneapolis with Regina!"

"Oh, dear," my mother said. "That explains why she kept calling last night."

"She went to Althea's this morning," I reported breathlessly. "But she wasn't supposed to! And Marge is going over there tonight to get her, and it sounds like it's going to be a pretty big disaster!"

"Do you think," my father asked, "that there's anything you could do?"

"Me?" I said. "What could *I* do?"

"Could you talk to Regina before her mother does?" he suggested. "Maybe try to help her make some sense out of the situation?"

"Me?" I asked again. Then I began to scurry around the house, looking for my shoes and socks. My father and mother watched me, their faces troubled. My own mind was a blank; the anger I had been feeling toward Regina had numbed me.

"I won't be gone long," I said at the door.

"Why don't you let me come with you?" my mother asked suddenly, and ran for her purse.

"I can't have her come," I whispered to my father. "I won't be able to help if she does."

"Go on ahead, then," he advised. "I'll talk to her."

And I slipped away.

Fifteen

When I got to their house, David and Althea were rocking together on the porch swing. Althea looked unusually pale, her face sagging with worry. Beside her David seemed equally troubled, but more agitated, his body leaning toward his mother protectively. He saw me first and sat up straight, beckoning me, his expression hopeful.

"Hello, David," I called. "Is she here?"

"Is she ever," David called back. He pointed up. I must have looked confused.

"She's upstairs, Arly," Althea announced sadly.

"She locked herself in the studio," David added.

"Oh, no!" I said, climbing the steps of the porch. "How long has she been up there?"

"Since Mother told her she couldn't live here," David said. "How long ago was that, Mother?"

"It seems like days ago," Althea said wanly.

"I just talked to Hilda," I reported. "I think Regina's mother is coming over here to get her."

"The more the merrier," David said under his breath.

Althea winced and stopped rocking. "She's coming here now?" she asked me. She covered her eyes with one small thin hand.

"I thought maybe I could talk to Regina before her mother got here," I said. They both looked at me so eagerly that I added softly, "But don't forget she hasn't listened to me in a long time."

"She needs to listen to someone," Althea said. "I'm afraid I've misled her somewhat about what I can do for her." She shook her head. "I truly never thought anything like this would happen."

David patted her shoulders comfortingly. "Arly will talk to her, Mom," he said gently. He gave me an encouraging nod and I nodded back, bracing myself. At that moment an unfamiliar car pulled up and stopped in front of the Dolores house. We watched Marge Miller climb out from behind the wheel. She approached the porch grimly, her head lowered, trudging toward us. At the bottom of the stairs, she looked up accusingly.

"Oh, Mrs. Miller," Althea said breathlessly. "Please come in."

She put her hand on Marge's arm and drew her through the front door and into the living room. David followed the two women, but I stayed on the porch, watching from the open front door. When Althea led Marge toward the sofa, Marge drew back. She looked older and more worn, but there was something determined about her round face. Her eyes were flashing. I had seen Regina's eyes flash that way.

"Where is she?" Marge asked.

"She's upstairs," Althea said nervously. "She'll be down in a minute. Maybe you and I should talk. I'm sure that together we can work this out—"

"Oh, you're *sure*, are you?" Marge interrupted angrily. She rummaged through her purse for a handkerchief and wiped her brow, struggling to catch her breath. "I wish I could be so sure."

Althea tried to begin again. "Regina thinks—"

"Mrs. Dolores, do *you* think that I want to stand here and listen to you tell me what *my daughter* thinks?"

"Of course you don't," Althea said. "It's only because she's been confiding in me lately . . . I thought perhaps together we could find a way to help her accept your decision."

At this, Marge looked suddenly on the verge of tears. "I know it's been hard for her," she said sorrowfully. "I know how she feels about moving again. But I have to do *something*." Then she seemed to remember why she had come to Althea's, and her face hardened again.

"Mrs. Miller," Althea faltered, "I know how you must feel—"

"Oh, *do* you? Do you know that, too, Mrs. Dolores?" Marge stood facing Althea, her expression defiant. "Let me tell you some things about Regina that I don't think you know. Some things that only I know."

She took a deep breath.

"I've been fighting for that girl from the moment she was born. She was not supposed to happen at all, you know. Our family was supposed to be finished. Then I had to protect her from her father wanting her to be a son. And I protected her from her sisters— they were older and different, not as sensitive—and they teased her and left her out of things. We were close then, Mrs. Dolores; we were important to each other. But when she started growing up and began to hate all the moving and to want things to be different in her life, it wasn't her father she turned on. Not him, who never paid any attention to her and who left her at the worst possible time, not him. It wasn't her sisters, either. No, it was me, Mrs. Dolores. I was the big, number-one problem in her life—everything was my fault. Then she got it into her head that I wasn't her mother at all—how could I be? I'm nothing to her. She tells me nothing, she asks me for nothing. Do you have any idea how it makes me feel to always hear what she's doing from other people?"

Althea and David were both listening, their faces grave. Marge looked from one to the other and took a deep, shuddering breath.

Her eyes wandered about the room. "Where is she?" she asked again.

Althea looked utterly miserable. "I'm afraid," she said, "that she's locked herself into my studio."

Marge's eyes widened at this news. "Well, then go up and tell her to come down at once!" she demanded.

Althea and David looked at each other helplessly, and the room swelled with confusion. I found myself trembling.

But then suddenly, unexpectedly, Marge lowered herself to the couch and began to cry. Althea sat beside her and took one arm, her own face tearful.

"Oh, well, I'll just go. I'll go now," Marge was saying brokenly. David came forward and made a move to help her stand.

I slipped away, heading for the safety of the ravines. I felt like I'd been holding my breath for hours, and as I ran I took long drafts of the still-hot August night, trying to clear my head.

It was dusk, still light enough for me to find my way along the path that Regina and I had traveled together in May. And thinking back to those earlier weeks I had a sort of revelation. I remembered the surprise I'd felt months ago, when I'd first learned from Ed Watkins that David was fatherless. And I also remembered my mother's offhand remarks about Regina looking like her father. My mind jumped to the many photographs of David's father in the rooms of the Dolores house, beautiful photographs. Suddenly, I felt the absolute and relentless absence of Regina's father so deeply that a huge emptiness opened around me. And almost instantly, this emptiness was filled with a waterfall of love for my own obtuse and utterly present father and for my dear, meddlesome mother, and I realized then that Regina had in many ways been right to suspect that I wouldn't understand her plight. We were in different straits, different worlds, and I reeled at this insight into how difficult her life had been compared to my own.

Then I realized that no one else knew what I knew about Regina—not Marge, not Althea—for I had become her shadow that summer. David had seemed sure that I could help. I would have to say something that she would really hear, really listen to. It would be difficult. And it would cost me her friendship forever. But I had to try.

So I went back the way I'd come, back to the third ravine and around the block, back to the porch again. Marge's car was gone, and David and Althea were still sitting in the swing, slightly illuminated by the streetlamp.

"She's back!" David said when he saw me. "Thank goodness."

"Arly, thank goodness," Althea echoed.

"I needed a minute to think," I explained. "But now I'm ready to talk to her."

"I'm so glad," Althea breathed. "I was about to go up and try again myself."

"I won't be up there long," I said. "But afterward, Regina may need a ride home." I added softly, "She won't want to come with me."

"Oh, of course, Arly," Althea said. "Of course I'll drive her home. You know that I never wanted any of this to happen, don't you?"

"Yes," I assured her. And then David and I exchanged a glance.

"Good luck," he said softly.

I waited at the door of the studio, hesitating a moment after announcing myself. Regina let me in. She had been sitting on the floor of the studio, on a pile of Althea's quilted pillows. After she let me in, she went back to the pillows and put her head down. She looked tired, but calm.

"Did you know that your Mom was here?" I asked.

"I saw her car pull up. What did she say?"

"She didn't say much. She left after a few minutes. She was pretty upset."

"*She's* upset. Have you heard what she's trying to do to *me*?"

I nodded.

"What did Althea say to Marge?" Regina asked.

"She didn't know what to say."

Regina threw up her hands. "I've been trying all day to get her to realize how serious this is for me. She doesn't seem to understand that I just *can't* go back to Minneapolis now. How can I convince her?"

She sat up and looked at me intently. "Has David been saying anything to her? I think I could get through to her if it wasn't for him, making her feel—" She stopped, and her face lit up hopefully.

"Arly!" she cried. "*You* could talk to her. You could tell her that you don't think I could *possibly* go away—"

"I don't think so, Regina," I protested softly.

"She likes you. They *both* like you. They'd listen to you, I just *know* it!"

I tried again. "You can't stay here, Regina. It isn't David's fault. I think you should go home now and just leave Althea and David alone."

Regina heard this and she looked at me, shocked.

"I think you should go home right this minute and work things out with your real mother."

Regina opened her mouth to protest, but I kept going. "You know she *is* your real mother, Regina. Saying she isn't doesn't change anything. And no matter how wonderful Althea is, Marge is your mother and it's not right to say she isn't and to be so mean to her and to blame her for everything you don't like about your life!" I stopped to take a breath.

Regina's face had changed—she was furious. "Get out of here," she said fiercely.

"I won't go yet," I said. My own anger had surfaced. "You can't tell me to go. This whole thing, this whole house, everything here used to be mine, Regina, so quit telling me when to come and when to go."

"What do you mean, *yours*!" Regina cried. "I thought we were friends—"

"We *were* friends. Until you met Althea and stopped caring about me or listening to me or thinking about what I might ever want to do! I don't know why I let you drag me around all these weeks, messing things up for everybody, confusing everything, taking what doesn't belong to you and all the time blaming your mother!"

Regina's eyes had filled with tears. "I can't believe you're saying this to me!" she cried. "All this time I thought you understood. Why were you always saying you *did*—"

"I was trying to be your friend, Regina, but whenever we would start to disagree, you would quit listening. But I thought all along that the way you were treating your mother was *terrible!*"

Regina's mouth fell open. "You said you *understood!*" she thundered. She was wiping her tears furiously; they spattered around her like rain. "Don't you see that I can't leave what I have here now? I can't leave Althea! I *hate* Marge!"

"I don't see why you hate her so much," I shouted back, although I was crying now, too. "I don't even believe you hate her as much as you say you do. Why don't you ever say you hate your dad—he's the one who left you in the first place. He's the one who moved you all around when you were growing up. He's the one—"

Regina covered her ears. "Shut up!" she screamed. "Shut up and get out of here. You're a liar—all this time acting like you're my friend. You've been listening to Marge and *she's* a liar. Get out or I'll . . . I'll call the *police!*" These words came out with such a hysterical shriek that the ridiculousness of her threat struck us both at once and we began to laugh wildly through our tears. Then something moved me to her side and we hugged each other crazily for a moment, before we remembered how far apart we had become. We both pulled away, and the room hummed with silence. Regina began to cry softly again.

"Please go," she begged.

"All right," I said. "I will. But I meant every word. And Regina, I *did* try to be your friend."

I ran from the studio, down the stairs and back out to the porch. Althea and David stood up and waited for me to speak. I took a deep breath.

"I think," I reported numbly, "that Regina will go home in a little while."

"You've been a good friend to her," Althea said, the words filling me with sadness. "I only wish I had been a little less blind."

I leaned against a pillar, feeling suddenly as though my legs would never carry me home.

"The car's in front, Arly," said David quietly. "I'll give you a ride home and then Mom can take Regina."

"I can walk," I protested.

"It's late, Arly," Althea said. "We're all exhausted. None of us were expecting any of this tonight. Please let David take you home."

I nodded. David stood up and walked down the front steps and I followed him. I climbed into the car and closed the door, pressing my head against the seat wearily.

Here I am, I thought. *Alone in his car and it's the*

worst night of my life. I watched his hands on the wheel and wondered if he was driving me away from his house forever. *Do something,* I told myself. *Tell him something.* But my head was a blur.

David broke the silence. "We could hear you both shouting in the studio," he said. He sighed. "God, things got out of hand so fast, didn't they?"

"Yes," I whispered.

"Do you think it will work out for Regina?" he asked.

It was such a complicated question; it made my head swim. I closed my eyes, fumbling for a reply. When I opened them, we were already past downtown. *Six blocks,* I thought. *Five blocks.*

"I mean, will the two of you still be friends, Arly?"

"I doubt it," I admitted sadly.

"You'll have other friends," David said.

It was the same thing my mother had told me just a few nights ago, but I knew from all my days of following David that he would not speak in a glib way about friendship. I knew how much of his life he spent alone. I looked at him, to see if I could be right in thinking that he had given me a compliment.

"It's not easy for me, making friends," I said.

He nodded understandingly. "But you have a lot to offer a friend, Arly. Don't worry if it just takes you a little longer."

I watched his profile, overwhelmed. *Three blocks,* I thought.

"Confronting Regina like that," David went on, "I know that must have taken courage." His arm came

142

across the seat and he touched my shoulder.

Then we were pulling up to my house and I was still trying to think of a way to tell him what he meant to me. He leaned away, and I heard the click of his door handle. Somehow I reached for his arm and tugged it, trying to find my voice. He leaned back toward me, and this movement brought our heads so unexpectedly close together that David smiled and cupped my cheek with his hand. I smiled, too, and then we kissed. It was very brief. We were both surprised. Then I opened the door on my side and slid away from him, still watching him; he looked a little embarrassed. When I was out of the car he opened his hand, still extended, and waved to me.

"Good night, now, Arly," he said.

"Good-bye," I whispered.

Then his car pulled away, leaving me in a daze in front of my house. The thought that I would probably not see him again pierced my heart and left me standing there a long time.

When I turned around, my father had come to the front door.

"Who drove you home?" he asked.

"Althea Dolores' son," I said. He held open the door. When I came in and collapsed onto the sofa, I noticed for the first time my mud-streaked legs from the ravine. I stood up and looked at myself in a mirror over our mantel; my face was also smudged, my eyes red. I groaned.

"David Dolores?" my father asked, watching me.

143

"He drove me home because I was so tired. I had it out with Regina, Dad."

My mother had come into the room. "Had it out?" she asked. "Is that as bad as it sounds, Arleena?"

I nodded. "I told her a lot of things I haven't been able to say before this. Like that I thought she was mean to her mother, and like I knew she didn't care about me very much anymore."

My parents exchanged surprised glances.

"It must have been hard for you to do that," my father said.

"What did Regina say?" my mother asked.

"She told me that I had never really been her friend." I bit my lip, tears coming back.

"Oh, honey," my mother said. "What a shame that all this had to happen now, with her leaving and everything."

"I'm glad she's leaving," I told them. "I didn't want to follow her around anymore."

They both nodded understandingly. "It sounds to me like Regina has a lot to settle in her own life before she could be the kind of friend you need, Arly," my father said gently.

I sighed. "What a night you've had," my mother exclaimed. "Let me run a bath for you." I followed her into the bathroom, wiping my eyes.

I sat in the tub a long time, running over in my mind all that had happened. Afterward, I sat on my bed watching an old movie. My father came quietly to the doorway of my bedroom.

"Arly?" he asked. I waited. "Arly, I just have one more question. About this boy, this David, who drove you home . . . ?"

I kept waiting.

"Ah, it just seems to me . . . was there something . . . was there a reason . . ." He stopped and looked at me, to see if I was going to help him. I didn't respond. He shook his head.

"Was there a boy involved in this somewhere?" he asked finally.

I just looked at him. After a moment I smiled at him through a few leftover tears.

"Oh, never mind then," he said. "Good night, kiddo."

Epilogue

Marge took Regina back to Minneapolis. David left soon afterward, to an East Coast college to study music. September came, and the events of the summer faded. I was in the eighth grade, I felt indescribably older, and I didn't want to be alone anymore.

Ed Watkins took a special interest in me with the oboe. I loved its solemn, passionate sound. I also had a naturalist class instead of the regular science class, taught by a young woman from Colorado who arranged a series of wonderful field trips. And there was another girl in this class that I began to like. Karla was shy, but she had a streak of dry humor. And she knew more about Michigan trees and plants than anyone I had ever met. We began to take long walks in the evenings together.

I still took walks by myself, too, but I was different. It had changed me to have memories, things that had started and ended in St. Martins. And though I still kept secrets from my mother and my father, they were secrets that it was a pleasure to keep, secrets without pain.

One afternoon, I was walking around town with Karla and we found ourselves, in a light snowfall, approaching Fireman Joseph. I got a rush of the old excitement as I stared up at him. I looked at Karla; she was gazing past the statue, watching the snow twirl into the river.

"Karla," I said, "this is my favorite statue in the whole world. I used to come here at night by myself, just to see it in the dark."

Karla looked up at Fireman Joseph with curiosity. Then she grimaced. "God, Arly," she said. "Sometimes you are really *morbid*."

It struck me then that if Regina had said that six months ago, I would have died. But that afternoon, I laughed.

"No offense," Karla said, laughing, too, "but give me a break."

I saw Althea occasionally walking through downtown, shopping, strolling in her leather boots, looking beautiful and always slightly out of place in St. Martins. She would smile and I would smile, and sometimes I would ask politely about David and his music. Then she would invite me to stop over to her house, knowing, I'm sure, that I would never come alone. I think we were both too uneasy about what had connected us during that summer, the way people feel when they know too much about each other.

I thought about Regina, especially on summer nights, wondering if she ever missed me, or if she would go through her entire life hating me. She probably thought I was knocking her when she was already down. I wondered if she had gotten over Althea, if it was better with Marge, if she would like Karla, if she had any new friends herself.

Then about two years later, my father came home from his music store on a Saturday and put a large envelope on the kitchen table.

"Something for you," he said. "From Althea Dolores. She brought it to the shop this morning. She said you could keep it; she has another."

I opened the envelope and pulled out a clipping from a Minneapolis newspaper. The headline read, "Sophomore Wins Citywide High School Art Contest," and beneath was a picture of Regina, looking slightly older and more glamorous, holding a large painting at her waist. On her left was the contest judge, holding a plaque, and on her right, with a beaming face, her plump hands clasped, was Marge.

"Wow," I breathed. "It's about Regina. She won some big art contest in Minneapolis."

"Althea said to pay special attention to the painting," my father said.

I squinted at it; it was hard to make out. It was quite unmistakably a painting of a house, but in wavy, soft lines as one would see it through water, or memories. The name of the painting was *Althea's House*.

My mother had suddenly appeared from nowhere and was reading over my shoulder.

"How about that," she commented.

"Did Althea say anything else?" I wondered. "Anything else about how Regina is?"

"She said she's had several letters, and she thinks that Regina is doing much better this year. She takes private painting lessons at the university. Looks like she's going to be quite an artist, doesn't it?"

I looked again at the photograph of Regina, at her smile, a dazzling, but slightly brittle smile, her gaze as piercing as ever. I felt a little accused by it.

"She writes letters to Althea?" I asked my father. "She's never sent anything to me."

"She sent Althea two clippings," he reminded me. "I think she wanted you to have one."

"It's so nice that her mother's there," my mother said. "Doesn't she look proud?"

I looked again at Marge. "She does," I agreed. I was glad to see it. Then as I glanced back at the painting, I felt a stirring of old sensations—that house, the ravines, an indelible glimpse of Althea and David through a window. Then I recalled an earlier image of David walking through St. Martins, and I saw myself following him, moving toward something I'd hoped would stretch me or fill me or give meaning to my changing life. When I looked back to Regina's face, I had softened; I felt grateful to her for reminding me of all that had happened that summer. I congratulated her silently, and she smiled back fiercely with her prize, her mother beside her and her painting in her arms.